Bug Muldoon and the Killer in the Rain

The toad whirled round with a strangled croak. It had forgotten all about me. There was no place on its face now for greed or anger. Its expression was stamped with one thing—fear.

My name's Muldoon, Bug Muldoon. I'm a private investigator in the Garden.

I was hoping for a bit of rest and recuperation after my last case. But it seems fate had other ideas for me. Fate, and the Thing that had sent the toad rushing from the Garden in terror. Next thing was, a hedgehog came crashing into Dixie's Bar and all hell broke loose. And when my pal Velma disappeared—well, what's a bug to do? I just had to go and look for her—and that meant a trip to the House. Would I find Velma there or had the Monster got her too? And who *was* this monster that had struck fear into the heart of the Garden? I was about to find out . . .

Paul Shipton grew up in Manchester and went to university in Cambridge. He spent several years teaching English as a foreign language before becoming an editor of school books in English and science.

He now works as a freelance writer and editor and lives in America with his wife and two daughters.

Bug Muldoon and the Killer in the Rain is his fourth book for Oxford University Press.

Bug Muldoon and
the Killer in the Rain

Bug Muldoon and
the Killer in the Rain

Paul Shipton

OXFORD
UNIVERSITY PRESS

OXFORD
UNIVERSITY PRESS

Great Clarendon Street, Oxford OX2 6DP

Oxford University Press is a department of the University of Oxford.
It furthers the University's objective of excellence in research, scholarship,
and education by publishing worldwide in

Oxford New York

Athens Auckland Bangkok Bogotá Buenos Aires Calcutta
Cape Town Chennai Dar es Salaam Delhi Florence Hong Kong Istanbul
Karachi Kuala Lumpur Madrid Melbourne Mexico City Mumbai
Nairobi Paris Sao Paulo Singapore Taipei Tokyo Toronto Warsaw

with associated companies in Berlin Ibadan

Oxford is registered trade mark of Oxford University Press
in the UK and in certain other countries

British Library Cataloguing in Publication Data available

ISBN 0 19 271837 1

1 3 5 7 9 10 8 6 4 2

Typeset by APS Image Setters Ltd, Glasgow

Printed and bound in Great Britain by Biddles Ltd
www.biddles.co.uk

For Auntie Pat and Uncle Ted

1

Death isn't fussy. It comes in lots of shapes and sizes in a
Garden like this. Sometimes it's the beak of a hungry
bird, sometimes the boot that descends from the skies.
Sometimes it wears the delicate threads of a lurking
spider. And sometimes good old Death has no pride and
rolls up in the shape of a big, warty old toad.

That's how it was today, just crouching over there in
the shade. The toad's golden eyes didn't blink. It was
acting cool, as if it hadn't noticed me. Only its pinprick
nostrils moved. It seemed unaware of everything.

Yeah, right.

I wasn't fooled. Its bulgy eyes were tracking me. That
deadly tongue was just biding its time inside a mouth that
stretched right across the toad's ugly mug. Just waiting
for yours truly to move into range. Then that lethal
weapon of a tongue would flick out and scoop me up with
its sticky coating. It would whip me back into that pit of a
mouth. And then all the toad had to do was swallow.

Well, it could try. Call me a dreamer, but I had other
plans for how the exchange would go. Right now I just
concentrated on playing my part—acted like I was the

tastiest beetle in the Garden. It wasn't hard. I've had plenty of practice dodging things that want to eat me. That's the way life is in this Garden of ours—you deal with it, or you end up as a light snack for something nasty.

Me, I'm nobody's light snack—not if I can help it. The name is Bug—Bug Muldoon. I'm a private investigator, and this nightmare of a Garden is the place I call home.

The toad job was the first I'd taken in a long while. I needed a break after a big case I worked some time ago. A treacherous group of ants had tried to hook up with the wasps and overthrow the whole order of the Garden. Things got pretty rough. In the end I found myself paying a visit on the biggest, meanest spider I'd seen in my life. It wasn't a social call, if you know what I mean. By the time it was over, I was still standing and the spider wasn't. But I got torn up pretty badly. Fact is, one of my wings still aches when the weather's damp. I try not to complain about it except when I'm in company.

When that case was over, I figured I ought to take things easy. Sure, I could carry on working as a private eye, but I wasn't going to take on anything dangerous from now on. I'd just handle the low-key stuff—you know, little cases where getting eaten wasn't on the daily list of Things to Avoid.

But now here I was, tootlin' on up closer to the toad. Don't go thinking I'd had a change of heart. I'm not one of those insects who's drawn to danger like a moth to a flame. A bug's gotta earn a living, is all.

So . . . the toad.

I'll tell you something about garden toads. They eat any kind of insect or worm they can get their tongues on, and they feed up to four times on a summer night. It gets worse—they have no teeth, which means they just swallow their prey whole.

Nice, huh? So you'd still be alive 'n' kicking as you slid down that pitch-black gullet. You'd just be sittin' in that belly as the digestive juices began to rain down on you. Thanks, but no thanks.

I stopped. This was close enough. Now it was all a matter of timing. If I got it wrong, then I'd be relaxing in that nice warm acid bath in the thing's gut.

I didn't need to worry. The toad wasn't lighting up the Garden with its blazing intelligence, and I played it like the sucker it was.

I inched forward and braced myself. An instant later the toad's tongue snaked out towards me like a bolt of pink lightning. I was ready. I ducked and rolled left. The giant tongue whipped across the top of my shell and scooped up the gunk that was coated there. The toad blinked at the horrible taste. It didn't know the half of it.

OK, time to make my move. I had to say my piece fast before that tongue came back for seconds. I kept it nice and simple. 'Listen up, toad!' I shouted. 'You oughtta be more careful what you eat. You just swallowed poison— a nice little cocktail of dangerous roots and leaves I threw together, then rolled in. It happens to be lethal to amphibians.'

The toad blinked again. It was as responsive as a rock, but I figured it got the gist. I went on. 'Pretty soon that poison's gonna be making its way round your whole body. And then you'd better believe that tongue of yours is going to be hanging out . . . but it won't be catching much of anything, if you know what I mean.' I paused for effect. The toad let out this little squeaker of a croak—*meep!* Its eyes narrowed in anger.

I got to the point fast. 'But there's an antidote . . . You interested?'

The toad gave a squelchy grunt. It was kinda disgusting, but I try not to let personal feelings get in the way of work.

'I'll take that as a yes,' I said. 'So . . . this is the deal . . . '

So far so good, and here's what I was going to explain. I'd give the toad the antidote to the poison on one condition—that it agreed to push off and find some other Garden to hang out in. That way the pond bugs who had hired me to do this job could relax and breathe easy— there'd be no more amphibian terrorizing them and gobbling up the mayfly larvae. Me, I'd pick up my fee for this nasty little afternoon's work, so I'd be happy. Heck, even the toad could squelch off into the sunset and enjoy whatever counts for a happy and healthy life among amphibians.

A no-lose situation, right? It sure seemed like a smart plan to me, but it's at moments like this that life socks you right between the eyes with the old sucker punch. See, I didn't get a chance to tell the toad any of this brilliant plan. Something must have sparked deep in the core of its dumb amphibian brain—something old and primitive and hissing that the only good bug was an eaten bug. The toad lunged forward and its tongue flicked out again.

WHAT? Hadn't it understood? Hadn't it believed me? These were interesting and valid questions that I couldn't give full consideration to. Not if I wanted to stay alive. That dumb old toad was going to eat me.

I rolled right and jumped up as high as my six legs let me. The tongue of death hurtled below. I almost landed right on top of it, but I managed to stay in the air an instant longer. That instant saved my shell. I landed safely and hit the ground running.

I charged towards the cover of a chrysanthemum bush. I could hear the toad letting out these wet chuckles behind me. It had good reason. It could cover the distance between us in a single hop.

Normally my best bet would have been to swallow my pride, point my head down, and dig to safety. That's what beetles do best. But it had been a dry season and the soil was baked hard. It would take too long for me to break through its crusty surface. I knew rain was coming later that day, but not soon enough to help now. No, I had to make it to the foliage. Burrow in as deeply as I could and hope for the best.

The sky darkened above me for a moment. It wasn't a cloud fleeting across the sun. It was Death dressed in slime. It was the toad hopping clear over me. Its plan— if you can use a term as grand as 'plan' for a pea-brained toad—its plan must have been to leap to the bush before me, spin round, and then open wide.

But that's when things got weird. The toad overshot and crashed into the bush up ahead. Then it just froze. It didn't turn round to greet me, eat me, or anything. It didn't let out even the quietest croak . . . Nothing. Its back legs trembled.

I just watched. What was going on? Why had—? Then I saw it. A sudden rustle in the bushes, though no wind had blown. There was something in there.

Before I had time to consider the matter further, the toad burst into action. It whirled around with a strangled croak. It had forgotten all about me. There was no place on its face now for greed or anger. Its expression was stamped with just one thing—fear. Total, all-consuming, I've-gotta-get-out-of-this-place-RIGHT-NOW fear.

It didn't even care where it went. It just had to get away.

So it did.

2

'So what was in there?' asked Velma.

'Beats me.'

The grasshopper stared in disbelief. 'Wait a minute, bub. You *did* go and see what was lurking in the bushes, right?'

'Are you kidding?' I answered. 'That toad was no buddy of mine, but I was happy to take its word. Something in those bushes scared the slime off it. I didn't need to find out what.' I stirred my sap and nectar with a pine needle and took a much-needed sip. It hit the spot. 'No, I just went and told the pond skaters that the toad wouldn't be bothering them again. Then I picked up my fee and came right here.'

Right here was Dixie's Bar. You could find me there most evenings. It was pretty early tonight but the joint was already full. We had to raise our voices over the hubbub of bugs around us. I'd forgotten it was fight night at Dixie's. That meant they had a pretty rough crowd in—there was a gang of wasps buzzing rowdily in the back, a cluster of nut weevils trying to prove they could hold their nectar, a gadfly bustling from table to table.

6

The place was standing room only—well, except for one empty corner, but that was no big shock when you saw the lone stinkfly sitting over there. Dixie, the club owner, was looking mighty happy. Nothing made the fat slug happier than a full house.

Velma shook her head and smiled. 'I don't get you, Bug. It'd drive me crazy not knowing what scared that toad away.' That's Velma for you. She's just about the best reporter there is in this Garden. Once that grasshopper gets a whiff of a news story, she won't let go. Must be her naturally enquiring mind. That was the big difference between the two of us. The only things I let *my* mind enquire about are, number one, what's for supper and, number two, how am I going to make it through another day in my preferred state (that is, undigested).

But Velma kept on firing those questions at me. 'But the toad won't have long to live anyway, will it? I mean, the poison . . . '

Normally I don't give away the tricks of my trade, but things are different where Velma's concerned. 'There *was* no poison,' I told her. 'It was all a bluff, see, to get rid of the toad. The stuff on my back was just some harmless mixture that tasted terrible. I wanted to scare the toad into promising to stay away from the Garden. Then I'd have given it a fake antidote it didn't need in the first place. See?'

'Pretty slick,' commented Velma. She had some slick moves of her own, so I took it as a compliment.

'I have moments,' I said.

The grasshopper leaned forward. Her compound eyes looked right into mine. 'But what's to stop ol' toady from coming back again?'

It was a good question but I knew better. 'You didn't see the look on that thing's face, Velma. If you had, you'd know. It won't be coming back.'

'Which brings us back to what was in that bush,' said the grasshopper.

I didn't say anything. I guess I could have told Velma that I'd stared into the depths of that bush for several long minutes. Nothing had stirred, and yet I couldn't shake the feeling that there was something in there. Something *different*. Something you wouldn't normally find in a Garden like ours, and it was looking back at me. It was hard to explain, just a tingle of fear in my antennae, but I've learned there are only two kinds of bugs who ignore feelings like that—dumb ones and dead ones. I could have told Velma the thought that had slipped across my mind, which was that I'd been right—Death *was* in the Garden this afternoon, but it wasn't in the form of a toad after all. It was hiding in the shadows of a chrysanthemum bush. It was in there waiting for me, only I didn't want to play.

Yeah, I could have told Velma all of this, but who wants to listen to that kind of talk when you're supposed to be relaxing with a drink or two? I just shrugged.

Velma wouldn't let it lie. 'You're not really so unconcerned, deep-down . . . are you, Bug?'

What could I say? Smart guys in my line of work don't get concerned unless they're being paid to. It might not be so nice, but who says the truth has to come all wrapped up with a pink bow?

As it turned out, I didn't need to say anything, 'cause Dixie the slug had slimed his way to the centre of the club. Everyone was careful not to tread in the silvery trail behind him.

The crowd fell silent and Dixie kicked off the evening's entertainment. On fight night, the stage area was roped off for the evening and became the ring. Bugs from all over the Garden crowded round it. The waiters scurried frantically trying to keep up with everyone's order. They worked fast—the crowd could turn ugly on fight night.

'Ladeeez and GENtlemen,' Dixie announced. 'Welcome to fight night!'

There was some cheering from a bunch of click beetles coming on tough, but the hard-core fight fans stayed quiet. They kept that way right through the opening bout—two tiny springtails who hopped and sprang around the ring like fanatics and hardly laid a tarsus on each other. It ended in a draw, and the two hopped off together for a drink like they were best pals.

While we waited for the next fight, I asked Velma about the news story she was working on.

'It's an in-depth feature about the Humans in the House,' she explained, trying to fake some enthusiasm for the subject. 'A couple of new ones have turned up. We think they might be visiting the Man in the House.' Velma challenged me to make some smart crack. I knew better, but I couldn't stop a laugh from sneaking out.

'What's so funny?' demanded the grasshopper.

I didn't want to offend my friend, who's a fine reporter, so I chose my words carefully. 'Every time news is slow, that editor of yours asks for a feature story about Humans. You know, what they're really like, whether they really have thoughts and feelings just like us. All that jazz.' I guess quite a few insects are interested in that kind of thing, especially those who live near the House. There's always a market for Human-watching stories in the news, but I'm not part of it. Humans are a mystery to me and I'm happy to let 'em stay that way.

'OK, OK,' admitted Velma. 'So I won't be breaking any big stories with this one. I guess news is always slow when MayDay is coming up.'

I nodded. Like everyone else, I was counting off the days to MayDay. It was the Garden's biggest celebration of the year. It was the only break in the day-in, day-out slog of fighting to stay alive. As the days got hotter and hotter, it seemed as if everyone was waiting for MayDay.

Back in the ring, a squat little sheep-tick was announcing the weights of the next two fighters. It was top of the bill, a bout between two stag beetles. The defending champion was a local boy. The challenger came from another garden, a beetle by the name of Moose.

'Now *that* is one big beetle,' Velma said when she saw the challenger. 'Why would any insect be crazy enough to step into the ring with him, let alone start fighting?'

I would have agreed, only this wasn't the first time I'd seen ol' Moose. I knew him from way back when. 'I give him about twenty seconds into the first before he hits the deck,' I said.

Velma wasn't convinced. 'The only thing that could stop *him* is a forestful of army ants.'

I pointed out a skinny silverfish who was standing near the ring. A knot of insects stood around him, all jostling to get closer. 'See that guy?' I said. 'He's called Slippery Pete and he lives up to the name. He's taking bets on the fight right now. Moose is his boy.'

Velma's slender antennae twitched at the scent of a story. 'I get it,' she said. 'A bunch of punters place bets on Moose to win, then the big lug takes a dive.'

I smiled. Velma caught on fast. 'You got it. Then the silverfish cleans up. It's a neat little scam.'

A bluebottle rang the bell for round one, and the two bulky beetles squared off. Things started slowly with lots of feinting and not much action. Stag beetles aren't too fast. Their fights are all about size and strength. Each one tries to lock the opponent in its jaws, lift it up, and then flip it over.

Both fighters made a couple of exploratory moves with their giant branching jaws, but neither one got much of a grip.

'Fascinating,' muttered Velma drily. 'Next time I'll stay home and watch the grass grow.'

I grinned. 'What do you mean? This is the noble art. I love it!'

Velma snorted. 'Yeah, right! Weren't you just saying the fight is rigged? How noble is *that*?'

'I wasn't talking about the boxing,' I said. 'I meant the noble art of pulling off the scam. That's what I'm interested in. Otherwise it's just two beetles long on muscle and short on brain, duking it out.'

Velma took a sip of her honeydew. 'You sure know how to show a gal a good time, Bug,' she said.

I wasn't even watching the action in the ring. I kept my eye on Slippery Pete—in particular, the long, bristle-like feelers that silverfish have behind them.

'Watch the little creep's tail,' I said to Velma. 'Unless Pete has changed his ways, you could always tell when the little creep was pulling a scam. His tail kinda twirls just a little. It's a dead give-away.'

Sure enough, halfway into the first round, the feelers at the silverfish's tail rose and twirled. The movement was so slight you'd never have noticed if you weren't looking for it.

'There it is. He's gonna make his move,' I murmured, and I was right. Moments later the little silverfish tipped good ol' Moose the nod. Right away the big beetle slowed down even more. His acting skills hadn't improved since I last saw him in the ring. He dropped his guard leaving himself wide-open. Now his opponent would have no problem gripping the top part of Moose's body and flipping him out of the ring. The scam looked obvious to me—about as obvious as the old response to the fungus-gnat's question. (You know, the fungus-gnat wants to know why nobody likes it. The answer is: *of course* nobody likes it. It's a fungus-gnat, isn't it?)

Not many of the other punters seemed to notice, except Velma, but then Velma is smarter than your average insect. The defending champ had lifted Moose in the air now. The fight was nearly over and the crowd was going nuts.

And that's when a non-insect cry ripped through the air, and things went really crazy.

3

There was just a second or two to hear the drumming of feet over the sound of rain outside, and then a giant creature burst through the line of rhubarb stems that formed one of Dixie's walls. It was a hedgehog—dangerous enough at the best of times, but this one looked wild. Its jaws were snapping madly at the air.

I'll tell you something about hedgehogs—they aren't fussy what they eat. The place exploded into action. Bugs were scurrying everywhere to get out of the creature's path. Those insects that could fly took to the air, but there wasn't enough room in the cramped bar and lots of them smacked together in angry mid-air collisions.

There was a whole lot of pushing and shoving going on, and soon Velma was no longer by my side. I wasn't too worried. She's been in enough tough spots to know how to handle herself.

I was more worried about Moose. Just before the hedgehog had crashed into the club—without an invitation, I might add—the other stag beetle had flipped Moose onto his back. Now the big beetle was unable to right himself. Of course, Slippery Pete was nowhere to be seen, and the crazed hedgehog was headed right for the helpless beetle in the ring.

Don't go thinking what I did next was any kind of heroics. Moose wasn't ever much of a friend, though I wouldn't call him an enemy—we sort of knew each other from the old days, that's all. Maybe I was just in the right place at the right time. Whatever, I rushed forward and grabbed hold of the big guy's wing case. I began to haul him back as fast as I could. It wasn't easy. Like Velma said, Moose was one big beetle.

I tried not to look up, because I knew what I would see if I did. That hedgehog was making one terrible din. I could feel its hot, mammalian breath blowing around the club like an angry whirlwind. I pulled harder, wondering why Moose had never considered watching his weight.

Waves of rain were gusting in now through the shattered wall. The hedgehog towered over us. It let out a final cry and fell forward. I pulled one last time and yanked the stag beetle clear just an instant before the hedgehog's head landed. Its quivering jaws were millimetres away from Moose. The mammal's eyes stared glassily ahead.

Moose shifted in my grip. 'Hey, Bug,' the stag beetle drawled. 'Good to see ya.'

It wasn't easy, but I flipped Moose back up the right way. The two of us just stood there waiting for panic to relax its noisy grip on everyone around us. It took a while. Even after a few minutes, confusion was still guest of honour at Dixie's Bar. No one was sure what was going on, and a lot of bugs were shouting and running around in circles. Perhaps it made them feel better. Dixie was doing his best to calm everyone down, but no one paid much attention to the slug. Most of them didn't stop to take in the obvious, which was this.

The hedgehog was a goner.

I wasn't crying any tears for it—too many hedgehogs had almost munched me too many times. But, hey, I could be big about this. I hoped it had gone on to hedgehog heaven, or wherever it is that bug-chomping, spiky-backed mammals go when they die.

'I've been to a lot of wild parties at Dixie's,' I said, 'but I never saw anything gate-crash like that before.' I nodded towards the unmoving hedgehog. 'What was it thinking?'

Moose lacked my natural interest in the inner workings of the hedgehog brain. He was too busy watching all the confusion. 'Just like old times, huh, Bug?' said the big beetle appreciatively.

'Yeah.' That was about as far as I wanted to discuss the good old days. But then curiosity got the better of me.

'So you're still working with Pete?' I asked. I wasn't surprised that the creepy little silverfish still hadn't reappeared. I bet he had crawled away through some crack at the first sign of danger.

The stag beetle shrugged. 'Yeah, but we don't pull the fight scam so much these days. Not like we used to. You know, Slade's got some big plans for the gang these days.'

The very word made me freeze. Slade. It was a name I hadn't heard in a long time. If I'd had my way, I would have gone a lot longer without hearing it. I said nothing. Moose wasn't the smartest, but even he picked up on the vibes.

'I thought you and Slade were buddies?' he said.

I nodded quickly. '*Were.*' There wasn't much else to say. I hadn't seen the cockroach known as Slade in a long, long time. Of course, I heard news of him now and then. It was hard not to. Slade was a big shot in the House now. When he said jump, a lot of bugs jumped.

The only thing was, my days of jumping to another

insect's orders were over. That's the beauty of being self-employed.

I looked over the top of Moose's bulky shell and saw that Dixie had managed to restore some sort of order to the club. I glimpsed Velma over at the entrance, talking to the bouncers. I had to smile. She was probably interviewing the two leatherjackets about what they had seen of the hedgehog. She's a reporter through and through, that Velma, from the tip of her antennae to the end of her abdomen.

'Gee, I'd love to scurry down memory lane a little more, Moose,' I said, 'but I guess I should lend a hand here.'

The stag beetle was looking around too. 'Yeah, yeah—and, you know, I ought to find Pete too.' There was no point telling the big lug that by now Slippery Pete was probably curled up, all nice and snug, in some dark little hole in the wall back at the House.

Moose lumbered off into the crowd, but he paused and looked back.

'Hey, Bug?'

'Yeah?'

'Thanks . . . for, you know . . . '

'Yeah.'

'And Bug?'

'Yeah?'

'Is there anything you'd like me to tell Slade? A message or something?'

I thought for a moment. A message did float into my brain but I told myself off for even knowing such bad words. I thought another moment or two before saying, 'Tell Slade that Bug says . . . just tell him that the greenfly's fine. OK?'

Moose didn't do a great job of hiding his puzzlement. 'I don't get it, Bug.'

I smiled patiently. Moose was one of those guys doomed to go through life never quite getting it.

'That's OK,' I said. 'Slade will understand.'

I turned and pushed my way through the crowd. It took a while but finally I made my way over to Dixie. I'd seen the fat slug looking better. He looked as if he'd just been given a salt shower.

'How's it going, Dix?' I asked.

'Swell,' answered the slug bitterly. 'Considering a crazed mammal just ripped up the club and nearly squashed the paying customers, that is.'

I was trying to think of a suitably sympathetic line, when one of Dixie's waitresses bustled up. 'Er, Dixie, there's someone here,' said the earwig. 'She's a survivor—the only one we found. We're not sure what to do with her . . . '

Dixie and I looked down. Standing behind the earwig-waitress was a flea. She wasn't very old and she looked bewildered. Suddenly I realized where she had come from—the hedgehog.

Dixie is a savvy businessbug, but some situations are out of his range. The slug offered me this pleading look and like a mug I fell for it.

I put on my nicest, kid-friendly voice. 'How ya doing, kid?' I asked, trying to come on like Uncle Bug or something.

It wasn't a tough question, but there was no answer from the flea. Her eyes seemed to be focused on something way beyond me. I tried again. 'What are you lookin' at?'

Fleas don't have good eyesight—they don't need it in the forest of hairs on a host animal's body—but this kid just went on staring off into the distance.

I tried one more time. 'I guess you were on that hedgehog, huh? What happened? What did you see?'

For a second I thought the flea looked my way, but then her gaze floated off again.

I was getting tired of this game. 'Listen, kid, if you want to find your way home, you'd better wise up and start talking.'

Just then I became aware of another bug at my side. Velma.

'That's a nice soft touch you have with bugs in shock,' the grasshopper said. I didn't know what she was getting at.

'I'll take care of this,' said Velma briskly. She ushered the tiny flea over to a corner and began talking to her in a low voice.

Meanwhile a small crowd of mixed insects had pushed their way up to Dixie. Like I said, you get a rough crowd in on fight night, and this bunch didn't look too happy. They were crowding round the slug and hopping up and down and saying stuff like:

'What are you going to do about that hedgehog?'

And:

'How can you guarantee something like this won't happen again, eh?'

And:

'It's nearly MayDay, you know.'

While Dixie did his best to stop the crowd from becoming an angry mob, Velma hopped back over with the flea. The small crowd fell quiet. Velma can have that effect.

'She can't remember anything,' announced the grasshopper. 'Says her name is Netta.'

'I thought you said she can't remember *anything*?' I said.

'She can't remember anything about what happened tonight, smart guy.'

The flea still had that pathetic, sort of dazed look. It gave the crowd what they were looking for—an outlet for their overheated emotions. At first they were all sympathy:

'Aaah, just look.'

'Poor little tyke.'

'I bet she's never been away from her host animal like this before.'

But, as these situations sometimes go, their comments gradually cranked up a notch and became harsher:

'So what are you going to do about it, Dixie?'

'What about the poor kid's friends?'

'Yeah. Someone's got to help her find the other fleas that were on that hedgehog.'

'It happened in your club, Dixie, so you're responsible.'

The crowd was getting fired up. This didn't look good. The slug's slimy mouth was working silently. I knew his head was full of calculations. Dixie doesn't like to spend money, but he's smart enough to know that sometimes you have no choice. Right now the big slug figured it would be money well spent if he could prevent a riot in his club.

'OK, OK,' he shouted glumly. 'I'll make sure she gets home.' He turned towards me. 'Bug, you'll handle the job, won't you?'

I could feel the hot stare of a lot of bugs drilling into me, but one look at that lost little flea didn't fill me with enthusiasm.

'Sorry, Dix. I'm a private detective, not a baby-sitter.'

But Dixie didn't get where he is today without being one smart business guy. 'I'll pay twice your usual fee,' he said instantly.

Bingo. Words like that swell my heart with thoughts of invertebrate kindness. I looked down at Netta. 'Come on, kid,' I said. 'A joint like this is no place for a young flea like you.'

Netta the flea said nothing.

4

When we got to my office, times had changed. I had begun to look back fondly on the good old days, half an hour earlier, when Netta hadn't said a word.

She had started to talk not long after we left Dixie's, and now the bug wouldn't stop. I can't say I'd ever hung out with many fleas before, but I'd heard plenty about them. As far as I knew, they were good for two things— jumping and talking. Netta wasn't doing much jumping, but she made up for it big-time with the talking.

This was her first time off a host animal, and it had made the little parasite dizzy with excitement. She peered at everything in open-mouthed wonder, and she talked about it all, non-stop and at length. 'What's this?' 'How about that?' 'I never realized!' 'Ooh!' 'Aah!' and all that. She didn't seem too cut up about being out in the big, wild world all on her own. It was like some great big adventure for her. The poor kid didn't know any better.

Right now she was saying, 'I don't want to trouble you, Bug—Mr Muldoon, that is—but I think I'm starting to get a little hungry, it's been a while since I had a bite to eat, you know—' And so on. You get the idea.

I looked around the office. As usual, there wasn't a lot of food lying around. 'I don't suppose some privet leaf would hit the spot?'

Her thin giggle bounced around the stem-walls of my office. 'Oh, that's a good one. Yes, very funny, Bug, sorry, Mr Muldoon. Is it OK if I call you Bug, though? I'm just so excited, you know, I've never spent any time off ship before. Feels a bit weird, actually. And no, to answer your question, I'm afraid I couldn't eat leaf. Blood's the thing for me, you see, a drop of the old thick 'n' red, that's what we used to call it back on the—'

She stopped as suddenly as a midge hitting a car windscreen. I enjoyed the silence for a moment, then asked, 'Back on the what? The hedgehog?'

It was like throwing a switch, *CLICK!* Netta got that dazed, faraway look on her mug again.

'Er, I . . . I . . . don't remember,' she said at last.

It was hard to believe. 'You can't remember *anything* about what happened tonight?'

'No,' she said in a hollow voice. It was one of those lost little voices that make you want to go, 'Don't worry, it'll all be OK,' or some such lie. Call me a softy—I said it.

But then Netta went and blew it all by perking up again and laughing. 'Isn't that odd, Mr Mul—oops—isn't that odd, Bug? I mean, I can remember my name and everything. My name is Netta. See? I told you! I can remember that I grew up on a cat. Lovely thick tortoise-shell coat, it had. Then I spent a few months on a squirrel, but I never really felt at home up in the trees, and all those nuts give the blood a funny after-taste. So I moved onto a hedgehog, not too long ago actually. I've been on that ship ever since, but . . . '

She looked around her blankly.

'But now you're not.' I thought I'd better break the

news gently. 'Because the hedgehog is a stiff. Dead. And you have no idea how that happened?'

Her empty look said it all. This wasn't going to be as easy as I'd thought. Netta had been the only survivor found, but I knew she hadn't been alone on the hedgehog. Fleas never travel alone. Her friends must have jumped ship before she did. But when? And where?

The weather wasn't working in our favour. Normally I would simply have followed the hedgehog's tracks back, but the rain had washed them to mud by now. No, if we were going to get Netta back with her friends, she would have to start remembering something about what had happened.

But this flea wasn't going to remember *anything* without a little prompting. Well, that was OK—I knew right where we could get some expert help.

'Get some rest,' I said to the flea. I pointed to the leaf in the corner. 'You take the bed. I'll be fine here. We've got a long journey tomorrow.'

'Where are we going?' I could tell excitement and fear were fighting it out for control of Netta's brain.

I settled back against an acorn and tried to get comfortable. 'We're going to see a bug about a bug,' I said. 'Goodnight.'

I didn't sleep much that night, and it wasn't just the lumpy acorn that kept me awake. Something Velma had said kept rattling around my mind like a springtail in a tin bucket. It had been just before I left Dixie's with Netta in tow. Velma had hopped over to me.

'Listen, Bug.' The grasshopper's voice was low and urgent. She glanced down quickly at the flea by my side, making sure the kid wasn't listening. 'This is a big story, I can *feel* it. I don't know why exactly—it's just a gut feeling and sometimes that's all there is to go on. But I know one thing—I've never seen a hedgehog flip out like

that before. It doesn't make sense. Unless . . . ' She looked
out through the broken walls, as if there might still be
something out there hiding in the rain.

'But what could do *that* to a hedgehog?' she wondered
aloud. 'A Garden snake?'

I shook my head. 'There hasn't been a viper in the
Garden for years.'

'What do you think then, Bug?'

If I'd stopped to think about it, I would have chosen my
words more carefully. I would have realized that this was
one of those moments when Velma's worldview and mine
bumped up against each other. My friend was looking for
the truth—I was looking to get by. I should have trodden
carefully.

I didn't.

'What do I think?' I said. I nodded down at the young
flea. 'I think I need to take care of this job and then pick
up a nice fat fee from Dixie. I can't see that the rest of it
is any of my business.'

Sure, part of me wondered what had happened to the
hedgehog. But, like I told you, smart guys in my line of
work only act on their curiosity when there's a cash
incentive; otherwise we keep our antennae out of things.
Velma was another matter—she was on fire with
curiosity.

'Well, I'm going to make it *my* business,' she said with
one of her determined looks. 'I'm going to find out what's
going on. The Garden public has a right to know.'

I didn't waste my breath telling her to be careful. Being
careful comes with the territory in Velma's line of work
and the last thing I would want to do is insult her
professionalism. Velma's a big girl, she knows the score.

The grasshopper leaned forward. 'Do me one favour,
Bug. Take care of this job for Dixie, find where the other
fleas are . . . ' Her big eyes were back on mine. 'But if

you can find Netta's friends, you'll probably find out something about what happened tonight. If you do, let me know—that's all I ask.'

Those had been the last words Velma had said to me. As she hopped off into the night, I couldn't help wondering if her voice hadn't held a note of something I didn't usually detect. Disappointment? What had she asked me earlier that evening—was I really so unconcerned about everything? It was a tough one and no answer was presenting itself now. But hours later, here I was in the middle of the night, listening to a tiny flea chatter away in her sleep and wondering why I had this feeling that maybe Velma was onto something. Perhaps something *was* very, very wrong in the Garden? I finally fell asleep in the early hours and my dreams were filled with snapping jaws and the cold, unblinking stare of something in the chrysanthemums.

Netta and I set off early the next morning. I don't mean crack-of-dawn early, but the sun was a lot lower in the east than I usually got to see. It wasn't a welcome sight, but I wanted to take care of this job and be done by morning's end.

Netta was raring to go. If she was scared about being out in the open, it didn't show. She was hopping up and down excitedly on those mighty back legs. 'It all looks so different, Bug, when you're not on ship, I mean, and looking through all those hairs. I never imagined . . . ' She kept on with that kind of stuff, and plenty of it.

We headed off south across the Garden. Every so often I glanced up at the sky. 'It's lovely, isn't it?' Netta gasped. 'All that blue. I think it's wonderful, and the fresh air? Oh my goodness!'

I didn't tell her I was looking out for any birds who might not have had their fill of early worms yet. I didn't want to put a crimp in the day by being swallowed before breakfast.

As it turned out, I didn't see any birds, but there *was* something unusual in the Garden. It was a Human, over on the east side of the lawn. It was well out of our way, but I made sure that we hugged the west border as closely as possible.

It's hard even to take in something as immense as a Human, but I did my best to keep an eye on this one. It was crouching down, looking at the grass. It held something in its hand, but I had no idea what. I'm not much of a Human-watcher, but I could tell this one was young. Not that this really mattered. It's not as if young Humans look all that different from the adults. They don't undergo metamorphosis, not even partial. They don't shed their skins, as far as I know, though some of them lose that hair stuff off the top of their heads.

Here's what I don't get about Humans. They have all their strong, protective bones on the inside, and lots of soft, squishy stuff on the outside. What kind of design is that? It didn't make much sense to my way of thinking— though, if I'm gonna be honest, I didn't use up a whole lot of thought on the matter.

To me the Human in the Garden was nothing more than the subject of mild curiosity. For Netta it was something else—it was a great big bag of blood. A giant container full of the old thick 'n' red. She couldn't see too well, but even at this distance the flea could catch a whiff of the Human.

'Oooh, you know I really am getting very hungry now,' she babbled. 'Perhaps if we hop over, I could just grab a quick bite to eat? You know—hop on, fill up the old tanks, hop off . . . '

I didn't slow down. 'Sorry, Netta. You'll have to eat later.' I wasn't dumb enough to wander over to a Human, even a young one. 'Come on,' I said. 'We've got a long way to go.'

Seeing that Human had made me think again about what Velma was up to. It sounded like it might be dangerous, and here I was not helping one bit. I forced down a surge of guilt. Velma knew the score, I reminded myself. Her line of work had led her into plenty of dangerous situations before this. She knew what she was doing when she abandoned her feature article on Humans and went looking for a 'real story'.

But what was the story? Though she wasn't even sure what it was, her reporter's instinct told her it had something to do with the hedgehog. Which meant something to do with this flea by my side too . . .

Except the flea *wasn't* by my side. I sighed and looked around. She was back a ways, getting ready to leap. At first Netta had done an OK job of sticking with me, but it was hard for her to keep her hops small enough.

The problem with fleas is—well, there are lots of problems with fleas, but I'm thinking of one in particular. They just can't travel like normal insects. See, usually they spend all their time just hitching a ride on their host animals. The idea of deciding to go from point A to point B is unknown to them. They just go wherever they're taken. No responsibility. When they get hungry, there's no problem 'cause their mode of transport is also their lunch. They only have to move when something important is about to happen, like the host animal taking a dip in the river or something. That's when they make their amazing leaps to safety. Then they just sit tight until they can hop back onto another host.

The bottom line was that Netta simply wasn't able to hop alongside me. She just couldn't do it. Like most fleas, the kid could jump over two hundred times her own length. That's a neat trick, but it's kinda hard to control. She'd have to hold back while I scurried along across the lawn. Then she'd let loose with one of those huge jumps, leap way over me and land far ahead. And then she'd wait until I caught up, and she'd do the whole thing all over again.

It was asking for trouble. This Garden is no picnic, especially for any bug that doesn't know how to handle itself. I kept shouting to the flea not to jump so far ahead. I might as well have told the sky to pack up and take a day off.

It wasn't long into the journey before trouble hit. Netta had bounded too far ahead of me yet again. There was a dandelion stem in my way and I couldn't see exactly what was going on, but I saw that the flea had landed near some insect poking up out of the ground. Then I heard a rough voice—'Hey, kid. Come 'ere.'— and my blood ran cold.

I tried to shout a warning, but I was too late. I pelted forward. The insect poking out of the ground was gone. I'd only glimpsed it for a second, but a second was all it took to know that this was bad news. It was a tiger beetle larva. That was bad enough, but here was the really bad part.

It had taken Netta with it.

5

If you ever find yourself wandering the Garden, take my advice—don't hang out with any tiger beetle larvae. They're a nasty combination of tough, mean, and very, very hungry. What they do is, they dig themselves a big old pit straight down in the soil. Then they slide in and anchor themselves to the sides. Only their head sticks out, resting at an angle to the rest of the body. And then they just sit and wait, until some nice juicy little bug comes along. Then they seize it with their sabre-like jaws and drag it down into the pit. And then . . . well, then it's dinnertime.

Except I wasn't going to let this creep dine on a client of mine. I had seconds to act. I raced forward, pushed my head down and began digging. I was lucky—the soil was soft after last night's rain. I barrelled through it, slicing down at a diagonal. My aim was good, and the tunnel intersected with the middle of the tiger beetle larva's vertical pit.

My jaws were level with the larva's soft gut. No time to lose. I jabbed a mandible at it and shouted good and loud so I could be heard through the soil.

'D'ya feel this, pal?'

There was a bellow of anger from somewhere above. I took that as a yes. 'This is a stinger and it's pointed right your way. Let the flea go or you won't be reaching metamorphosis.'

More muffled shouting, getting angrier now. Tiger beetle larvae aren't known for their mellow approach to life. I carried on, jabbing as hard as I could and coming on strong with the tough guy patter. 'You're wondering what I am, huh? Yeah, I bet there's just one question gnawing away at your little larva brain. Is this really a loaded stinger poking in your belly, or am I bluffing? Well, that's for you to decide, punk. But you'd better decide fast, 'cause I'm getting bored. And when I get bored, bugs start dying.' OK, maybe I laid it on a little thick, but you get no points for being subtle in this Garden.

The larva's shouting died down, as it tried to wrap its brain around this unexpected problem. It was a tight fit, but at last the insect made its mind up.

The next thing I heard was a sort of 'WHEEEEH!' sound from up above. It was Netta leaping to freedom. The larva had fallen for it! Sometimes the bluff works, but I didn't have time to sit back and bask in the warm glow of my success. Not when I was so close to one of the Garden's meanest predators. I backed up quickly, pulled a 180 and scooted up to the surface.

I took in the situation topside as quickly as I could. Netta was looking dazed, but unhurt and out of harm's way. The tiger beetle larva's armour-plated head was back out of its pit. It twisted round to look at me, its simple eyes balls of contempt.

'I *knew* you were bluffing,' it spat. 'I *knew* it.' It rocked back and forth as if it was trying to wriggle free of its pit. 'Come back here, you!'

I was at a safe distance, so I smiled pleasantly. 'Better luck next time, junior.' I turned my attention to the flea. She looked bewildered.

'I think from now on you'd better ride on my back,' I said. 'Hop over here.'

The flea jumped onto the hard shell-casing on my back and we set off again. For a long while we could still hear the tiger beetle larva behind us. He was shouting and ranting, a lot of juicy stuff about how we'd meet again when he was a fully grown tiger beetle, and all that. That larva had kind of a fresh mouth on him, but it was nothing I hadn't heard before.

Netta was trying to take in what had happened. Because of her direct hook-up from brain to mouth, this meant I got to listen. 'Well, that wasn't very nice, was it?' she was saying. 'I mean, I don't know how things work on the Outside, but I can tell you that fleas have a certain code of conduct on board ship. That larva fellow didn't seem like such a bad sort to me, a bit of a stick-in-the-mud, perhaps, but—' And so on.

It took me a while to catch on—the flea was criticizing my manners. This was rich! She hadn't even understood the danger she had been in. At one point there was a lull in the stream of talk. Enough time for me to say what was on my mind, which wasn't much. Only the truth:

'That "larva fellow" was going to eat you.'

I let that one sink in, then I added, 'Tiger beetle larvae are the pits.'

Netta thought about this for a long moment. All she said was, 'Oh.'

I pressed on. We were almost at the end of the Garden now. We had crossed the final soil-bed and were at the fence that marks the far boundary of the Garden. I looked out into the meadow beyond.

'We're heading into wild territory now,' I told the flea on my back. 'Better hold on tight.'

I crossed under the Garden fence and then struck out south-west for the woods. The grass was untrimmed out here and the going was harder. Up and down over clumps of grass, up and down. Uncaring as ever, the sun climbed steadily, and the day was getting hot. MayDay would be coming soon, no doubt about it.

Netta's spirits were picking up again slowly, and she began to return to her old talkative ways. 'Are we nearly there? Because I'm not sure how long I can go now without a bite to eat, you know I've got to keep my energy up, I'm a growing flea . . . ' And so on. I tried to tune the torrent of words out, but a sudden expectant silence told me the flea had just asked a question. My luck was in and she repeated it.

'I said, why don't we just fly there, Mr Bug? It would take a lot less time, wouldn't it? I mean, beetles *can* fly, can't they? And you *are* a beetle, aren't you?' She said more stuff too, but that was the gist of it.

Silently I debated how much to tell her. At last I said, 'I got my wing pretty ripped up in a case I did a while back.' That was all she needed to know. I didn't tell her this had happened while I was running for my life from the biggest spider this side of the Rain Forest. At the time I'd thought that the beast had pulled my wing clean off. I guess it wasn't quite so bad, but now one of my wings wasn't in such great shape. My flying was even wobblier than it used to be, and I no longer took to the air if I could help it. The truth was, I was afraid to, though you wouldn't catch me telling a gossip-crazy flea that.

'What's the matter?' I asked. 'Just sit back and enjoy the ride. Not too far to go now.'

We were approaching the edge of the woods. I scanned the horizon nervously. The last thing I wanted to run into was a gang of robber flies. That was another reason why it made sense to stick on the ground.

We passed into the shade of the trees. I hadn't been here for some time, and I took a moment to get my bearings. I looked around. That's when I realized we weren't alone. There was an insect on the tree up ahead. Of course, there are a lot of bugs in the world and you never know what you're going to run into. There's no reason why we shouldn't have come across some spiffy red admiral butterfly who could have utterly charmed my companion and left her thinking that the great outdoors was an altogether splendid place. The only thing is, the slender bug on the tree was no red admiral.

It was an ichneumon wasp, tapping away at the bark with her antennae. Her long ovipositor—the needle-like tube for laying eggs—hovered threateningly in the breeze.

A spark of anger flared in my thorax. 'Hop off for a moment,' I said to Netta. The flea started asking why, but she hopped off as well.

'Hey!' I called up to the wasp. 'Beat it, sister. Scram.'

The wasp glanced down. If looks were stingers, I'd have been flat on my back with six legs twitching. I guess she was weighing up how serious I was. Then, once she saw that I meant business, I guess she was weighing up what her chances were in a little one-on-one combat. It took a while but finally she decided it wasn't worth the risk. She gave a little tut of disgust and flew off. She must have figured she could always find another tree. The sad part is, she was right.

Of course, Netta had plenty to say about the incident. 'Well, that wasn't very polite, now was it, Mr Bug? I mean that poor insect was just sitting there harmlessly, did you really have to say those things? I can't see what it had to do with us, frankly, I mean—' And so on.

I explained, mainly to shut the flea up. 'That was an ichneumon wasp, and you're right—it didn't have anything to do with us. I just don't like ichneumon wasps. They've got this sneaky way of giving their eggs the best start in life. What one does, see, she sniffs out the eggs of another species of wasp. Then she pokes her ovipositor through the bark and lays her eggs right next to the other wasp's eggs.'

Perhaps Netta could see what was coming, but I spelt it out. 'Well, by and by, the ichneumon's eggs hatch, and guess what their first meal is?' I watched the flea's face as the penny dropped.

'You mean they . . . ?'

'You got it—they eat the unhatched eggs of the other wasp.'

Of course, this was perfectly natural. I knew that. All we insects have evolved different ways of getting through this life, and so on and so forth. Fine. Just don't ask me to like all of it. Call me old-fashioned—I don't think that's any way for a mother to act.

All Netta said was 'Oh'. It was her second 'oh' of the day, and this one came out sounding even more puzzled than the first. You had to feel sorry for the kid—sooner or later every bug's got to learn that it's a hard world out here, but that doesn't mean it's a nice job being the one who doles out the lesson.

We finished the rest of the journey in silence. We'd had a busy social day, what with the tiger beetle larva and the ichneumon wasp. The excitement must have tired us out. The woods were filled with buzzes and clicks and cheeps and all that kind of stuff. I guess there were plenty of predators around who might fancy a little flea for starters and for the main course one beetle who looked slightly the worse for wear. I *guess* they were around, but we were lucky and we didn't run into any.

At last we stepped out of a patch of sunlight and into the shade of an oak.

'We're here,' I said.

'Where?'

I nodded at the rotten log in front of us. 'You're about to see the smartest insect you'll ever meet.'

6

The Professor is unique. A real one-off. He's a book louse, but not just any old book louse. He spent most of his life in a place Humans call a 'library'. Like most of his kind, he lived on a steady diet of the paste in these things called books. The big difference was, the Professor was hatched on something called an encyclopedia—that's a book about everything in the world, or so the Professor says.

The other unique thing about the Professor is this: whatever he munched his way through, he absorbed that knowledge. Don't ask me how it worked, it just did. And, of course, this diet gave him a more rounded education than your average bug. What I'm saying is—the Prof was smart, OK?

You might have expected an academic bug like that to live out the rest of his days in the comfort of the library, right? Wrong. Not the Professor. One day he found himself staring out of the window and wondering what things were like out here. He got to thinking, which is what the Prof does best.

Eventually, he made up his mind. He'd had enough of

the indoors life. He got a mosquito to fly outside with a general message requesting assistance. It made its way to me, which was a lucky break for the Prof—there are plenty of bugs out here who'd be happy to strike a deal with a book louse and then not keep their side of the bargain. The Prof is book-smart, but he isn't all that Garden-smart, if you know what I mean.

Well, to cut a long story short, I flew over and helped the Professor get out of that library. He had a pretty good idea of the sort of place he wanted to settle in, and I knew that the woods near our Garden would fit the bill.

That had been months ago, and this was the first time I had returned to the rotten log the Professor now called home. I still remembered the way in. It was a tight squeeze under that log, but I pushed through. Netta followed.

It was dark under there, and it didn't look as if the Professor had done much to spruce the place up.

He must have heard us coming, 'cause the book louse scurried out to greet us. Like I said, lots of book-smarts, no Garden-smarts. We could have been anything looking for a mid-morning snack.

'My dear Bug!' cried the Professor happily. 'How splendid to see you! Quite, quite splendid!' Judging from this hearty welcome I guessed he didn't get much company out here. From what I hear, the conversation of wood lice doesn't sparkle.

'Hey, Prof. How you getting on?'

The louse nodded vigorously. 'Oh, fine, fine! Um, yes, splendid! I'm getting on splendidly, my boy. '

'And how are you doing with those big questions of yours?'

The Professor nodded several times more, as if he had something urgent to say, but no words found their way to his mouth. Who knows what he was thinking? That's what the Professor did out here—he thought. That's all, just a whole lotta thinking, all day long. You know, all about the big questions like . . . Why are we all here? What's the purpose of life? What's the meaning? Did the world really hatch from a Cosmic Beetle Egg? All that kind of baloney. The Prof had wanted to come out here to do it, he said, because he was looking for 'wisdom instead of mere knowledge'. Me, I wouldn't go looking for wisdom underneath a dead old log, but then my thoughts run no deeper than a raindrop on cement. The way I see it, if you let your thoughts run too deep, you might just drown in them. Who knows? Maybe the Professor was a good swimmer.

Whatever.

I nudged Netta forward. The spring was still missing in the flea's step. She looked hungry and unhappy.

'Professor, this is Netta. She's a—'

'Yes, of course! *Ctenocephalides felis!* Enchanted to meet you, quite enchanted.' The Professor was beaming away. 'Yes, yes, a fascinating life cycle, that of the blood-sucking parasite. Of course, the species of siphonaptera with which I am most familiar—'

I enjoy a biology lesson as much as the next bug, but I felt we'd better turn to the job in hand. 'What we're here for, Prof, we need your help with a little problem.'

'I want to go home,' said Netta miserably. These were the first words she'd uttered in some time.

'Yes, yes, of course! The homing instinct and all that. And how, um, how may I be of assistance?' asked the book louse. He did his best to mask his scientific curiosity with a look of sympathy.

I looked down at the two of them. The Professor wasn't much bigger than the flea, but that's where the similarity ended. Just one glance at Netta told you how strong and agile she was. In contrast, the book louse's greyish body was pale and soft. He had a couple of wing pads on his back, but they were useless—wings had long since vanished from his species. His eyes were weak, his mouth designed for chewing nothing more demanding than mould. All in all, he looked like a bug you'd want to have on your side in a debate, but not in a scrap. That was OK—I wasn't here to send the Professor into combat.

I explained the Netta situation quickly. As he listened, the book louse tapped his abdomen thoughtfully against the log. He went on thinking and tapping, tapping and thinking, for some time.

At last he spoke. A single triumphant word. 'Hypnosis.'

'Hip what?'

The Professor was too swept up to give me an answer. 'Yes, yes, my boy, we'll regress her, do you see? We'll regress her and then we'll be able to know everything she saw, right down to the very last detail.'

I can't say I understood it all, but I could follow the important part—the Professor knew a way to make Netta remember what had happened.

Here's how it worked. We all moved to the outer edge of the log, where there was more light. The Professor scurried off and returned with a tiny fragment of coloured glass. He asked Netta to look at the glass and nothing else and to listen to his voice. That's all there was to it.

Netta gave me a questioning look. I nodded that it was OK, and the Professor got cracking. He began to wave the green glass to and fro, at the same time moving it gently around so that it caught the sunlight. While he did this, the Prof went on and on, all this stuff about feeling sleepy and that. I didn't know about Netta, but it came close to doing the trick on me. I could easily have nodded off. The Professor's voice was no more than a whisper. Netta listened to its drone. Her eyes followed the glittering fragment.

'Back and forth, back and forth,' said the book louse. 'You are feeling so very, very sleepy. You are quite, quite relaxed. Your legs are relaxed. Your thorax is relaxed. Your antennae are—'

'Relaxed?' said Netta.

'Yes!' snapped the Professor. Then as calmly as he could: 'But I must ask you not to talk any further, my dear.'

It took only a few minutes more of the book louse droning on and on and waving his shiny bit of glass in front of the flea. Finally, the Professor turned to me.

'She's ready, my boy.'

I looked at Netta. Her eyes were open, but they weren't looking at anything. As far as I could tell, no one was home behind that gaze.

'Ready for what?' I asked the Professor. 'What's wrong with her?'

'She's hypnotized, my boy,' said the Professor. 'Quite, quite fascinating, really. It's a state in which the conscious mind—' He saw the look on my face. 'Well, perhaps you don't have to worry about the ins and outs of how it actually works, my boy.'

'So what now?' I asked.

'Ah, now it's time for our young friend to regress. We'll take her back in her mind, do you see, back to the events of last night at Dixie's establishment. And then . . . well, then we'll find out what happened to her jolly old host animal, the hedgehog.' The louse turned his attention back to the flea and cleared his throat. 'Can you hear me, Miss Netta?'

The flea gave a slow, solemn nod.

'I want you to tell us everything you can remember about what happened last night.'

7

There was a long silence. Then Netta began to speak, but what came out wasn't her usual excited gabble. She spoke slowly now and her voice sounded small and faraway. Something about it made me think of a tiny twig being carried away on a stream.

'The ship was sleeping in the bushes all afternoon,' she began. The Professor threw me a puzzled look. He knew all this fancy scientific stuff about fleas, but he didn't know too much about the way they think and talk. I explained quickly that fleas referred to their host animals as 'ships'.

Netta was unaware of my whispers. She went on. 'We had all drunk a big lunch and we decided to have a nap too, so—'

'Yes, yes, that's very good,' interrupted the Professor, 'but can you tell us what happened later, my dear? After the rain started . . . '

Netta blinked twice, as if she was resetting her brain to the right time. 'It was a wet evening and the ship was searching for food along the side of the House. It was dark. The rain was picking up, and we had all burrowed in deep to stay dry. Suddenly the ship stopped.'

Netta stopped too, and her eyes suddenly bulged with fear. When she began talking again, some of that fear had seeped into her voice. 'Some of the other fleas wanted to see what was going on, but I was nice and comfy, so I stayed put. But then the shouting started. I didn't know what was going on, but something was wrong, I could tell.' Netta's voice was picking up speed again. 'The ship was moving fast now. I didn't know if it was chasing something or running away. I jumped up to the end of one of the lookout spines and suddenly I was staring straight at—I—I was staring straight into the eyes of—'

I hunched forward. 'Into the eyes of what?'

'The eyes of a monster,' gasped Netta. 'It was horrible. It . . . it wasn't like anything I've ever seen before. I think the ship had attacked it, but the monster wasn't afraid, not one bit. It lunged at us. I knew the other fleas were all jumping off, abandoning ship, but I was too scared to move. The monster had turned away and it was making for the drainpipe on the House. The ship was moving fast in the other direction, and I could tell it was out of control. I closed my eyes and clung on to the spine for all I was worth. The ship crashed through one bush, then another, and then it collapsed. I was thrown clear, I think. I'm not really sure, it all happened so quickly. Then I opened my eyes and there were all these bugs rushing around me and asking if I was all right and what had happened, but . . . ' Without warning, Netta's head lolled back. The outburst had exhausted her.

The Professor and I looked at each other. 'Try to find out more about this monster,' I urged. 'What did it look like?'

The Professor tried, but it was no good. Netta mumbled something else about the thing looking horrible, and then her head slumped forward. The flea was done.

'What do you make of that, Prof?' I asked.

The book louse thought it over. 'It seems clear enough where her former companions are,' he answered at last. 'If they hopped off near the House, I guarantee they'll either be on a rat or on a cat, depending, I suppose, upon the type of household.'

'From what I've heard they've got both up at the House, and from what I know about Netta, her shipmates would go for the cat. But that isn't what I meant. What about this so-called monster?'

'Ah, yes,' said the Professor. 'Fascinating, my boy. Quite, quite fascinating. She certainly believes that what she saw was a . . . um . . . a monster. Of course, like my own species, fleas are not known for the keenness of their eyesight, and there is the very real possibility of optical illusions—'

The Professor launched into a detailed explanation, which I might have found fascinating if I'd understood a single word. But my mind was racing. Netta had seen *something*. I was sure of it. Whatever it was, it was something out of the ordinary and it was something dangerous. What else could explain the fate of that hedgehog?

A sudden thought slapped me right in the kisser.

Velma!

The grasshopper had sensed that something was up— that's why she had gone to look further into this story. Velma was one tough cookie, but a queasy feeling told me this wasn't like the usual situations we learn to live with in the Garden. There was the unmistakable whiff of extreme danger in the summer air . . . and Velma had gone searching for it.

But here I was, late in the morning and hundreds of metres away from the Garden. Anything might have happened and I was powerless to help.

I looked down at the sleeping flea. 'How long before she comes round?'

As it turned out, not long at all. Within a couple of minutes Netta's eyes had flickered open.

'What happened?' she murmured. 'What did you find out?'

'No time to explain,' I said. 'We've gotta get back to the Garden *now*.'

The Professor was pretty eager to have us stay a little longer—have nettle juice with him or something. You had to wonder if the Professor didn't find the company of his Big Thoughts just a bit boring at times.

'Another time, Prof,' I said. I had moved out from under the log. We didn't have much time. I thought a moment or two, then I turned to Netta. 'It'll take too long if we go on foot again. I'm going to fly us back.'

(I should have known better. Hadn't I given up flying? When you look back, it's easy enough to see the chain of mistakes that can lead you into danger. That was Mistake Number One, right there.)

Netta was still groggy from her hypnosis session. She nodded agreement and gripped onto the edge of my casing. I thanked the Professor for his help.

'Anything I can do to broaden the horizons of insect knowledge, my boy,' said the book louse with a flourish of his antenna.

It was time. I tried to act casual, as if it hadn't been weeks and weeks since I last dared to fly. OK, here went nothing. I opened my wings and flapped like crazy. Muscles that I hadn't used in way too long screamed their indignation. I told them to can it.

'Hold on tight,' I shouted to Netta. 'We're in for a bumpy ride.'

And then we were in the air. For a second or two we could hear the Professor's shouted farewells from below, and then a warm current lifted us beyond it. It wasn't the most graceful flight. Truth is, we were wobbling like a mosquito sprayed with DDT, but I figured we'd make it back in one piece.

Everything was swell for a good twenty seconds, thirty tops. If I'd been thinking straight, I guess I should have looped around the edge of the woods. I didn't. I just wanted to be back in the Garden fast, and I took the shortest route possible.

(That was Mistake Number Two.)

The sun was still beating down. It made it hard to see much of anything—especially the airborne figures that were hurtling out of the shadows to our left like two six-legged streaks of lightning. Robber flies!

Of course, I should never have tried to outfly them. I should have just dropped out the air like a stone, taken my chances on the ground. I didn't.

(You've guessed it—that was Mistake Number Three, and in my line of work you're lucky to get three strikes before you're out.)

And that's just what our luck was—all out.

8

The first robber fly hit with the force of a runaway Goliath beetle. POW! A blow like that was enough to send me spinning out of control, but that's not how robber flies operate. After they strike, they grab hold of their victims with powerful forelegs. Then they fly them back to their perch, stab them quickly with their snubby beaks, and then they begin to eat them.

Nice, huh?

The robber's grip was unbreakable. There was no point in struggling, so I just sat back. I can't say I enjoyed the ride, but at least I tried to use the time productively. That meant ordering my brain to throw a life raft of a plan onto the sea of panic sweeping over me. No luck. My brain picked a bad moment to turn mutinous, and the waves of fear came crashing down.

Robber flies go a lot faster than I can, and the world was a blur of greens and browns around us. And then suddenly it stopped. The robbers had landed on their perch, up high on the tip of a rosebush branch.

The one holding me let go. It figured we'd know there was no point in trying to escape. I guess we did. The sight on the leaf below didn't do anything to change my mind. It was littered with the dried-up exoskeletons of the robbers' previous victims.

'Nobody likes a messy eater, boys,' I said, trying to add a touch of humour to the situation. No dice—the robbers weren't in the market for comedy. These guys were professionals. They didn't waste their time on small talk. They began to edge towards us, taking their time as if they didn't want to spoil their supper with any unseemly struggling.

'Nothin' personal, pal,' commented one of them flatly.

'That's OK then,' I said. 'As long as it's nothin' personal, *bon appetit!*'

I didn't know if Netta fully understood the danger we were in, but the little flea knew we hadn't come here for afternoon tea. She knew something was wrong. She had hopped forward off my shell. I rested an antenna on her shoulder and tried to calm her shakes.

And that's when the rough and ready shape of a plan began to rise to the surface in my brain. It wasn't much, but it was all we had.

With my front leg I slightly adjusted the direction Netta was pointing in. The flea probably thought I was offering some kind of comfort. Maybe I was, but I was trying to buy us a chance to get out of this situation alive as well.

The robber flies were nearly upon us. It was now or never. I chose now.

'Jump!' I yelled.

Netta acted on pure instinct. Her mighty back legs sprang and she shot forward like an armour-plated rocket, spinning and tucking in her legs in the classic flea manner.

She hit the first robber fly full on. One moment he was sitting there just kinda working up an appetite. The next, he had been blasted clean off his leaf. The poor sap never knew what hit him.

It was a sweet moment—the kind that doesn't come along anything like often enough—but, as usual, there was no time to enjoy it. Not with the other robber fly still there, and not looking too happy about the twist events had taken lately. He was starting to snarl his anger. I guess things had become personal after all. They always do.

I knew I had to do something fast, but the question was—what? I'm no match for a robber fly one on one. We weren't out of danger yet. But there are times for thinking and there are times for acting. This wasn't a situation you could think your way out of, so I just put my head down and charged.

I never even reached the robber, and here's why. Netta. The flea had ricocheted straight up off the first robber. She landed back on the perch in a tight little ball of energy. Then, without hesitation and with perfect aim, she unleashed that energy again, springing forward a second time. This time I didn't have anything to do with it and it wasn't pure instinct either. It was a planned move and the flea played it perfectly. She hit the second robber head on, and it too plummeted from the leaf. The battle on the rosebush was over and we were still standing.

'Nice move,' I murmured.

Netta wasn't listening. She was panting hard. I reckoned the slightest breeze would set her off springing all over the place. She looked around in jerky movements, as if wondering where the next unknown danger might pop up from in this terrible place called the Outside.

'Let's get home,' I said to the flea.

It was a good suggestion, especially as there was no telling when those robber flies might be coming round.

Netta hopped back on top of me, and we half-jumped, half-glided down to the ground.

The next few minutes were a blur. I was done flying. I just pointed myself in the right direction and ran and ran. Grass below and sky above. I kept an ear out for the tell-tale whine of the robber flies looking for revenge. It never came, but I didn't let myself relax. (The Garden is full of insects who have relaxed themselves into oblivion.)

Soon the ground was beginning to look more and more familiar. We were getting close to the Garden again. Still I didn't stop.

Once we were back on my home turf, I didn't slow down. Maybe if I had done, I'd have noticed that something was wrong in the Garden. I was too focused on just getting to Dixie's. It was only later that I realized that the place was way too deserted for a sunny day like this. That meant folks were hiding underground, and there had to be a good reason for that.

I have no idea how long the rest of the trek took. I can tell you all six legs were aching by the end of the run. But then at last Netta and I were back in the fat slug's club. The flea was still looking sorry for herself. The poor kid was tired. Tired of this whole Garden, tired of the constant struggle of life off-ship. She was a long way from home.

I wasn't feeling too peppy either, even though Dixie's Bar is probably the closest thing to home for me. But right now there was trouble in the old homestead. I had sensed it as soon as we went in. Even in a quiet period, there's usually a pleasant buzz of activity in Dixie's place.

Not now. The main room was silent. Practically deserted. I didn't like this. I liked it even less when I saw who was waiting at the bar and talking to Dixie. It was a housefly by the name of Shaky Jake.

Don't get me wrong—Jake's a pal of mine. One of the best. I just wondered what kind of trouble had brought him here. You see, Jake didn't usually come to Dixie's. He preferred to get his kicks elsewhere. Fact is, Jake was a sugar-head. He had crash-landed in a sugar bowl one time, and since then he was heavily into the sweet, crystalline stuff. He spent most of his day searching for discarded bits of chocolate and gum. Energy food, he called it.

'B-b-bug, you're b-b-back,' the fly stammered. He gets like that sometimes when he hasn't had a sugar fix in a while. Gets the shakes too, which explains the nickname.

'Yeah, I'm back, but where's everyone else?' I gestured to the deserted club around us. 'Where's Velma?'

'There's big t-t-t-t . . . '

I was used to waiting for the end of words with Jake, but Dixie cut in. 'Big trouble,' said the slimy mollusc glumly. 'A lot's been happening round here.' I guess so. The slug didn't look too surprised that I still had Netta in tow. He didn't even ask about the case, which was pretty unusual when you considered that he was going to foot the bill. If Dixie wasn't checking up on his business concerns, then a lot really *had* been happening.

I didn't like the look of this. I knew I had to find out more, but something told me that Netta didn't need to hear what was about to be said. She had witnessed enough bad stuff lately. Why expose her to more?

'Hey, kid,' I said. 'Why don't you go and sit at one of the tables and have yourself a drink or something?'

'What if I don't want a drink?' pouted the flea. I couldn't blame her—she had plenty to pout about.

'Then go and sit at the table anyway.'

Netta took her time, but she did as I asked. When she was out of earshot, I turned back to the fly and the slug.

'Big trouble like what?'

'It all started after fight night,' began Dixie, 'not long after you left, Bug. We hadn't even straightened the place up when a couple of insects came in. They were ranting and raving about something they'd seen in the rain. Some kind of monster, they way they told it.'

I remembered the description Netta had given under hypnosis. She had used the same word. Monster.

'Why didn't you send someone to tell me?' I asked.

'Everyone thought these guys were crazy,' explained the slug. 'We reckoned they'd seen the hedgehog on the rampage and then let their imaginations do the rest. But then it turned out that a bunch of insects had gone missing from the Garden this morning . . . '

'That's when I f-found out, B-b-bug,' said Jake. 'I w-went to get you b-but you'd already l-l-left.'

'What does Velma reckon?' I asked.

'Nobody knows,' said the slug. The silence hung in the air like a spider's web in the breeze. Jake broke it at last.

'V-v-velma is one of the m-m-missing insects too, Bug.'

The information closed on me like the jaws of a predator. Velma had gone looking for trouble, and I guess she had found it. I had to do something and *fast*.

'So what's being done about it?'

With one antenna, the slug indicated the back room of the club. 'There's a meeting of the MayDay committee going on right now.'

'They're t-trying to decide w-w-what to d-d-d-do.' This news didn't fill me with confidence—the MayDay committee had trouble agreeing on what leaf to eat for lunch, let alone what action to take over something serious like this.

'Listen, Jake,' I said, 'I need to talk to the committee. I've some information that might help. But —' I nodded

my head towards the little flea. 'I need someone to keep
an eye on the kid for me. Keep her out of harm's way. Can
you do it?'

I didn't wait for an answer. I was already heading to the
back room where Dixie had said the MayDay Committee
was meeting.

'Sure thing, B-b-bug,' said the housefly.

9

Here's how the committee is *supposed* to work. Because MayDay is the only time in the Garden when all enmities are forgotten, it takes a lot of planning. Each year, a committee gets elected to do it. It's a multi-species committee, and every kind of insect in the Garden puts forward a representative to be a part of it. The idea is to ensure that no decision favours one species or order over another.

So much for theory. In practice, the committee spent most of its time bickering and arguing. And that was when they were doing no more than the usual preparations for MayDay.

But suddenly nothing was as usual. MayDay was being threatened by something that no one in the Garden even understood. This was a crisis far beyond the usual realm of the MayDay committee. I wasn't sure if they were up to the job.

When I entered the back room, the committee insects were crowding round to listen to a delegate from the ant colony. For an instant my hopes rose. Everyone knows the ants are the real power in this Garden. If there was a problem brewing, they were the ones who could sort it out. Several thousand of them, that is.

I didn't know this ant, but she was pretty high-ranking by the look of her. She gave me a nod of recognition, but she kept on speaking to the committee.

Yeah, my hopes were raised for all of about two seconds. Then I heard what the ant was saying, every word delivered in that deadpan way typical of the ants.

'As I explained,' the ant said, 'we are engaged in treaty negotiations with another ant colony. The Queen is personally involved in these negotiations, and we are unable to give assistance until they are completed . . . '

No surprise that this message didn't go down too well. A murmur of discontent rumbled around the room. A lacewing was getting pretty irate, and one ground beetle looked close to walking out. A bunch of other committee members tried reasoning with the ant. They might as well have tried spitting into a force-ten gale. Once the ants have made up their collective mind, they don't go back on it.

Thing is, I knew that the ants would have helped if they could—in that big case I told you about, I had done my bit to get the Ant Queen out of a tricky situation, and the whole Garden knew she owed us Garden-bugs a favour or two.

But in the ant world Inter-Garden relations were just about the most important thing the Colony ever did. I could see why—get things wrong and it could be full-blown war between two ant colonies. That would mean thousands upon thousands of casualties. Compared to that, a few missing insects meant nothing. The ants' decision wasn't a matter of morality, it was a matter of mathematics.

I lifted an antenna to be heard. The dragonfly who was chairing the meeting glared around the room and called for quiet, and the babble gradually faded. Lots of eyes turned my way, not many of them glowing with the warmth of insect friendliness.

I started talking and I didn't stop until I'd told them everything I knew. It didn't take long.

There was silence for a few seconds as the MayDay committee considered my account of what the young flea had seen. Then the babble started up again. I stood back and waited while the dragonfly quietened them down again. She was a tough old dame, and she managed to restore the meeting to order without too much trouble. Then she looked at me solemnly and asked, 'So what do you propose, Mr Muldoon?'

'Let's look at what we know, shall we?' I began. 'Number one: a bunch of insects are missing, right?' Nods all round. 'Number two: there's *something* in the Garden, and chances are, that something is what's behind all of these disappearances. We don't know exactly what it is, but we do know it's unusual-looking and it's dangerous. Just ask our friend the hedgehog . . . ' A tiger moth let out a harsh cackle at that, then stopped when he realized he was cackling alone.

'We know something else too,' I continued. 'Whatever this thing is, the flea saw it heading into the House. There's no guarantee that it's still there, but it's the only lead we have.'

I knew they weren't going to like the next bit—the majority of Garden insects don't like to stray into the House. Too many have strayed in there and never strayed out again.

'So . . . here's what you need to do. Get together a squad of insects, send them into the House and see what's in there . . . I generally work alone, but I'd be willing to come along too.' I didn't explain that I had personal reasons for wanting to join the expedition. They didn't need to know that one of the missing insects was a friend of mine.

I gave the idea time to sink in. It sounded as if the murmur of confusion was turning to one of approval. Maybe they were going to go for my plan? But then a sawfly piped up, 'Well, I think we should take a preliminary vote on Mr Muldoon's suggestion. Then we can move to a second vote tomorrow . . . ' Lots of heads nodded agreement.

'There isn't time for all of that,' I shouted. 'This is a state of emergency, or hadn't you noticed? We need to act now. Tomorrow may be too late.'

The dragonfly was glaring at me, and it was easy to see why dragonflies were one of the most feared predators in the Garden. If we weren't in a committee meeting on neutral territory like this, a lot of insects would be mighty uncomfortable to have a dragonfly glaring at them like that.

'We understand your concern, Mr Muldoon,' she said, the voice of authority. 'However, our hands are tied by the committee's rules of conduct. We simply do not have the authority to carry out your proposal in the time frame you have suggested.'

I couldn't believe this. 'Just so long as you follow your precious rules and regulations,' I said bitterly, 'I'm sure no one will mind about dying.'

'Sarcasm will get you nowhere, Mr Muldoon,' snapped the dragonfly. She was right—I'd used a lot of sarcasm in my time and nowhere was exactly where it had brought me. (So why did I keep on using it? Sentimental reasons, I guess.)

The deep-blue globes of the dragonfly's eyes were still on me. I knew something was going on behind them. At last, she got round to it. 'Of course, the committee would have no objection if a lone operator were to look into this matter first, while the committee studies the feasibility of putting together a cross-species expedition . . . '

I got the picture, but I wanted the dragonfly to say it. 'And who do you think would be dumb enough to take on a job like that, all alone?' I asked.

Her gaze never wavered. 'We would, of course, be willing to pay you,' said the dragonfly.

A boll weevil by her side leaned over and mumbled something, and the dragonfly quickly corrected herself. 'Well, of course, the committee would have to vote on the exact fee, but I'm sure we could meet your usual terms satisfactorily . . . '

I knew where this was going and I didn't like the trip. One thing was clear to me—I would have to take care of things on my own. 'Yeah, vote away,' I said, backing towards the door. 'Vote on what you can pay me. Take a vote on what you can do to help. Take a vote on how many leaf-stems to have in your next cup of nectar . . . '

I was out the door and gone, ignoring the indignant uproar in the room behind me. I left them to it. I had things to do.

The main area of the club was still as good as deserted. Jake and Netta were over in the far corner. That was one conversation I'd have loved to sit in on, under other circumstances. Another time . . . I kept my head low and went up to Dixie at the bar.

'Listen, Dix. Pass a message on to Jake for me, willya?'

'He's just right over there, Bug.'

'I know, but I want to make my exit without having to explain things to the flea. Just tell Jake Bug said to look after the kid a little while longer.'

I headed for the rear exit.

'Where you going?' asked Dixie.

'All things considered, where I'd *like* to be going is out to the lawn to catch me some sun. Where I *am* going is up to the Big House.' As a wise bug once said, you can't always get what you want.

Dixie's face said it all. The big slug knew all the rumours—how lots of Garden insects were afraid even to go near the House, how there'd been reports of vicious battles among the insect gangs that did live in there. It was generally agreed that the House was one bad place, and that was before anyone had mentioned that a monster might be hiding in there.

Dixie racked his brain for something appropriate to say. At last it came to him.

'Have a nice day,' said the slug.

10

I've heard talk of the towers termites can build. Giant, air-conditioned structures, they are, reaching proudly to the skies. The greatest architectural wonder of the insect world, and so on and so forth. Maybe I'll see one some day, but as I looked up at the House, I realized that it would take a whole lot of termites to build anything as impressive as this giant structure. It was bigger than a hundred beehives. I was still on the lawn and the thing filled my entire field of vision.

Well, somewhere inside it there had to be answers. Whatever it was that Netta had seen in the rain, it had headed towards the House. According to Dixie, Velma had planned to start her enquiries over here, too. One way or another, everything led to the House.

I started out across the patio. It had been a long time since I had been over this way, and I wasn't thrilled to be back. This place wasn't our world. I knew that plenty of insects spent most of their time inside the House, hardly ever venturing out, but, to my way of thinking, that was no way to live. This was the world of Humans. As far as I was concerned, they were welcome to it.

Up ahead was a window set into the outside of the
House at ground level. It led to the only part I had
ever seen, the Cellar. I got closer and climbed over
the metal guard that was set around the window. I
checked it over quickly, but there was no point of
entry here.

I was scuttling along to the next window when I heard
it, the unmistakable sound of a bug bouncing nearer.
Then a cry cut through the air—'Bug! Wait for me!' and
I was in no doubt who it was.

The flea landed in front of me. 'Fancy running into you
here,' I sighed. 'What are you doing, Netta?'

She looked pretty frantic and I could understand why.
It was a big enough deal for a flea to go travelling with
another insect. Now Netta had come bounding after me
all on her own. The kid was having a big day, and it was
taking its toll on her.

'Bug,' she gasped, 'I can't wait any longer, I'm starving,
you've *got* to let me come inside the House with you,
you've got—' And so on.

'Where's Jake?' I asked when I could get a word in.

'He found a boiled sweet over by the vegetable patch.
He told me he'd just be a moment, but I didn't stick
around. I took my chance and I jumped right here to find
you.'

I nodded. Jake was a good guy, but his judgement got a
little clouded when there was candy around. I couldn't
blame him—everyone has a weak spot, and sugar was
Jake's.

But that still left me with a flea-sized problem—Netta.
I didn't know what I was going to find inside that House.
It might be nothing, but I didn't want a flea hanging
around, just in case.

'Netta, I don't even know what I'm looking for in
there,' I told her. 'This is too dangerous, kid.'

The flea pulled herself up to her full height. 'Listen, Bug Muldoon . . . I've been off ship for I don't know how long and I haven't had a drop to eat. I was nearly eaten by a tiger beetle larva and when that didn't work out, I was nearly dinner for a couple of robber flies, so don't talk to me about danger . . . '

The flea had a point, I had to hand it to her. Who knew how long all this would take? Not me, but I did know one thing—the poor kid couldn't go much longer without food. Fact. And it wasn't as if the Garden wasn't already packed full of dangers behind every leaf.

I made my mind up. I knew I had to find Velma, but I had responsibilities to this flea as well. And maybe the two goals weren't so different. 'OK, kid, here's the deal,' I said. 'You can come along. We'll find the cat and drop you off with your pals, and then I've got business I need to take care of alone. But if for any reason things don't play out that way, then you've got to do exactly what I say. Deal?'

The flea was hopping with excitement. 'Deal, Bug!'

Part of me hissed that I was making a big mistake here, but I didn't have time to dwell on it. I headed for the next window and Netta followed. This one was more like it—a thin crack curved across the glass. Down at the bottom it broke into a spray of small cracks. Only one triangular hole looked big enough to squeeze through, but one was all we needed.

'Careful,' I warned. 'Those edges are sharp.'

Of course, it was no problem for the little flea to hop through. I had a bit more trouble, but I made it. We were inside. We stood a moment on the inner window ledge. I could feel the breeze from outside through the hole in the glass behind me. Once we moved away from that, we would be well and truly stuck in this dark, alien environment. Great.

I took a deep breath and started down the wall to the Cellar floor. Netta held on tight and soon we were back on the horizontal. We were behind the back of a big stack of Human objects. I had no idea what any of them were, but the layer of dust across everything told me that it wasn't anything the Humans used much. Just a load of junk they had thrown down here.

'What now?' whispered Netta. At the sound of her voice, something not too far away scuttled off on skinny legs. A crane fly? A daddy-long-legs? I didn't know and I didn't care. I would be happy if everything felt like scuttling away.

'The Cellar's the best way in,' I explained quietly, 'but I'm guessing we won't find the cat down here. We need to head upstairs.'

The stairs were over on the other side of the Cellar. We started out, scrambling over a stack of wood that had been cut into such unnaturally straight pieces you'd never know they had once been trees. It was on the second of these that we ran into our first indoors insect.

It was a reddish-brown beetle. It didn't look dangerous but you never know. I approached it carefully. 'How's it going, pal?'

I was about to ask if it had seen anything unusual in the last day or two. But then the beetle looked up and fixed me with a stare as intense as the midday sun. All my questions melted away under its glare.

'Where are you going?' the beetle demanded.

I didn't see what it mattered if I told the truth. 'Up the stairs and into the House.'

I guess it was the wrong answer. 'No . . . where are you going *in the wider sense?*'

I sighed. Why is nothing easy? 'In the wider sense . . . we're going up the stairs and into the House.'

'That's where you're wrong, pilgrim,' said the beetle

triumphantly. 'In the wider sense you're going where we're all going—the big D.' The beetle had the look of someone who thinks he has unlocked the secret of the universe. He was welcome to it.

Suddenly the beetle cocked its head to one side and froze. I deduced that he was listening to something— hey, I'm not a private detective for nothing.

'Shhh!' the beetle snapped. 'Got to keep quiet. Listen! Can you hear it?'

We all listened to absolutely nothing. OK, maybe I could hear the old house creaking around us, but somehow I knew that wasn't the right answer.

'There! You must have heard that!'

'No,' I said.

But then I realized there *was* a noise—a kind of far-off, sombre tapping, so faint you barely noticed it.

'Oh dear, oh dear, another one bites the dust!' declared the beetle, as if proving some important point in a debate. 'Got to pass the news along.' And with that the beetle jerked forward and began hammering its helmet-shaped head against the wood it stood on. *Tap, tap, tap, tap, tap!* It made my head pound just watching.

Seconds after he was done, we heard the faint sound of another tap-tapping in the distance. The message was being relayed.

'That's gotta hurt,' I said.

By way of an answer all the beetle said was, 'It's chalking up a good score this week.'

I didn't want to ask, but I knew I had to. 'What is?'

'Death!' declared the beetle with a knowing grin. 'The Big D's on a bit of a roll right now. Bugs dying left, right, and centre, and this House is the place for it.' He leaned forward. 'You might say this is Death's House . . . statisically speaking, that is,' he added with a conspiratorial wink.

I took a quick glance at Netta, who was shifting uncomfortably from leg to leg. This little chat wasn't doing much to lift her spirits. The fact is, it wasn't cheering me up a whole lot either.

'And why do you need to keep score?'

The beetle looked offended. 'Who's going to keep score if we don't?'

It was one of those questions that's trickier to answer than you think. I didn't touch it. Instead I started to back up and make our farewells. 'Well, it's been a blast but we've got to be on our way, so—'

The beetle had other things on his mind, namely whacking his head against the floor again. *Tap, tap, tap, tap, tap!*

Netta was watching with a blend of horror and curiosity, but I pulled her away. We moved on and the tapping got fainter and fainter behind us. Netta didn't speak until the sound was no more than a distant drumming.

Tap, tap, tap,

    tap, tap, tap,

       tap, tap,

         tap, tap

           tap . . .

The silence sounded sweet. 'It wasn't telling the truth . . . was it?' asked the flea at last. 'I mean about Death and all?'

'Don't worry,' I said, faking a calmness I didn't feel. 'House insects can be pretty weird. That was a death watch beetle. It was only living up to its name. They're all a bit on the morbid side.' Netta didn't seem convinced. I didn't bother telling her what I thought of the death watch beetles and their gruesome little count, which was this: sure, the insect mortality rate remained at a steady 100 per cent, but why dwell on it? I guess everyone needs a hobby.

'We've got to concentrate on the job in hand,' I went on, 'which means dropping you off on that house cat.' There'd be time then for me to snoop around, but I didn't have to let Netta in on that.

We carried on in silence for a while. Something about the place gave me the spooks. I knew it was a nice sunny day outside, but here in this artificial world it was twilight dark. The only light came from the two grimy windows at the top of the wall behind us. I didn't like walking on this concrete surface. I missed the feel of soil and grass under my feet. It's not that I'm a nature-lovin' boy or anything—I just know what the dangers are in the Garden and where they might be lurking. The hard, cold feel of this concrete told you that it would offer nowhere to hide in a crisis.

We had moved into another area of the Cellar and the stairs weren't too far off, when suddenly Netta yelled, 'Stop! . . . I can smell blood!'

I stopped. I knew that fleas had a good nose for the old thick 'n' red. This was even more true when they were hungry, and Netta hadn't sucked down a single drop of blood in a long, long while. I knew something else: this wasn't a good place to be if trouble went off. We were too far from the wall and whatever protection or cover its cracks and peeling paint might offer. We were way out in the open.

But then again, I couldn't hear anything. Not even the distant tapping of the death watch beetle. Maybe Netta was mistaken? I listened again.

Nothing.

'Are you sure?' I whispered.

'Yes, I am!' Netta hissed back. 'I'd know that smell anywhere.'

'The cat?' Netta shook her head, *no*.

OK, so where was this animal full of blood? Maybe Netta was so hungry she'd started to *imagine* she could smell food? Maybe she was going off her rocker? Maybe . . .

That's when I heard it. A squeak in the darkness. Something was coming.

11

The squeak was followed by other noises—the chatter of sharp teeth. The scratching of claws on concrete. These sounds weren't music to my ears.

'Quick!' I yelled. We scurried (in my case) and leapt (in Netta's) towards the wall. There was a tiny patch where the plaster had chipped away. It didn't offer much protection, but it was the only hiding place around.

We didn't get there with much time to spare. When I looked back into the open expanse of the cellar, there was movement in the darkness now. Even in the gloom, I could make them out. Over on the other side of the Cellar, they were. Two rats. They hadn't clocked us yet, and I didn't fancy finding out what would happen if they did. We pressed ourselves into the crack and waited and watched.

Don't go thinking that there are rats in every house. But the one near the Garden is a big old place, and the Man doesn't do too great a job of looking after it—or so I'm told by bugs who know about such things. Me, I have too many other things on my mind to go wondering about the living arrangements of assorted mammals.

'OK, Netta,' I whispered. 'Get ready to jump if one of them comes close enough, OK? You may not want to end up with a rat for a ship, but you may not have a choice. Riding on one has got to be better than being eaten by one.'

Netta nodded nervously. I knew she was thinking that all of her friends would be on the cat upstairs, not on some manky old rat creeping around in the cellar. 'But what about you, Bug?' she asked.

'I'll take my chances.'

The rats had made their way into the middle of the floor now. They looked nervy, ready for action. That's when rats are at their most dangerous. Instinctively I pushed myself further back against the brick of the wall. And then suddenly my antennae were going nuts. There was something dangerous here, but it wasn't the rats, it was something *else.* I whirled round, scanning the shadows along the wall for the tell-tale signs of spider web.

What I saw wasn't a spider. It was worse. It wasn't like anything I'd ever set eyes on before.

It had appeared from *somewhere,* further along the wall, and it was looking right at us. It was a monster.

OK, I guess I can be more specific. The thing was big—much bigger than me. It had these two huge, pincers on its front legs—they looked lethal—and its long, armoured back arched forward. At the end of its tail, dangling almost over its head, was a truly wicked-looking stinger. Death comes in a lot of shapes and sizes. Right now its pinprick eyes were trained on me and Netta.

The flea by my side hadn't budged. She had to be frozen with fear, just like me.

The monster raced forward. It was fast. Even if my brain had been co-operative enough to give me a sporting chance to get away, it wouldn't have done much good.

But the monster wasn't coming for us. It raced right by

me and out into the open arena of the cellar floor. Out to where the rats were foraging for scraps.

I've heard a lot of talk about rats. Some insects say they're pretty smart, others that they're your typical dumb vertebrates. I wouldn't like to come down on one side of the issue or the other, but I knew one thing. Those two rats in the Cellar were smart enough to know when they didn't stand a chance. They took one look at the thing coming towards them, snapping its pincers like a nightmare crab from hell. Their whiskers twitched in alarm. They both let out terrified squeaks, and then they ran like crazy, right back where they had come from.

That's exactly what I had in mind, a spot of running like crazy. I would have done it too. The only thing stopping me was a familiar voice. It came from further along the wall we were currently trying to press ourselves into.

'Hello, Bug. 'S been a long time . . . '

I'd know that voice anywhere.

'How's it going, Slade?' I asked.

The cockroach was squeezing out from a crack I hadn't even noticed. I may drop the odd complaint about the Garden, but I'm really an outdoor kinda beetle. There are lots of things about house-living I don't know anything about.

Slade was different. Even back when I knew him, he always liked coming up to the House. These days I don't think he ever left it. This was Slade's world.

He came closer. Slade was fast even for a cockroach and, let me tell you, that's fast—cockroaches can move it some when they want to.

He nodded towards Netta and smiled. 'I see you're running with a different crowd these days, Bug.'

I kept it professional. 'This is Netta. She's a client.' I didn't say more. I was dying to ask about Velma, but

that's not the way you play things with Slade. You've got
to let him think he's setting the pace.

By now a lot of other insects were creeping up around
us. No shock—I didn't expect Slade to wander too far
without his boys to back him up. It wasn't his style.
There were about twenty of them in all—a bunch of
other roaches, some earwigs, a couple of carpet beetles.
The biggest insect there was hanging back, but I caught
his eye and nodded.

'This is turning into a regular reunion,' I said. 'Didn't
think I'd see you again so soon, Moose.' OK, I wasn't
talking quantum physics, but the big stag beetle was
stumped for an answer.

'Yeah, yeah, that's right,' grinned Slade. His eyes
didn't leave mine. 'Moose said he ran into you at
the fight. Yeah, he told me you'd said to say the
greenfly's doing fine. I got a real laugh outta that,
Bug.'

As if to prove the point, he laughed again. I didn't join
in, but Slade didn't seem to mind laughing alone.

'Just so long as I bring a little joy into your life,' I said,
'I can feel it's all been worthwhile.'

Slade cut his laugh off dead. He was up so close to
me now his long antennae were nearly touching mine.
He gestured at the cellar around him as if it was some
kind of big deal. 'I bet you never thought of me as an
insect who could head up the biggest gang in the
House, huh?'

'You'd be surprised at how little I've thought of you at
all, Slade,' I answered.

The grin on the cockroach's mug was frozen in place,
but anger flashed across his eyes. It was gone when he
spoke again. 'I've missed having someone like you
around, Bug,' he declared at last. 'You know, someone
who can make a little conversation without his brain

turning to mush.' He looked around at his own boys sadly. 'Someone who can see the big picture.'

'Funny you should say that, Slade, 'cause I'd like to ask about that big picture. Only the picture isn't looking too nice from where I'm standing.'

I pointed to the middle of the cellar floor, where the monstrous creature stood alone. There wasn't a rat in sight.

Slade wanted to come on cool like a bigshot, but his grin stretched so big he nearly fell into it. 'Ah, you mean my secret weapon? Hold on a moment.' The cockroach turned to one of his earwig henchmen. 'Legs, go find Pete, willya?' he hissed. 'We can't just leave her out there in the open.'

The earwig didn't waste any time scurrying off to carry out Slade's orders. The cockroach turned his attention back to me. He hardly looked at Netta. 'It's an interesting story, Bug,' he said. 'You'll get a kick out of it.'

I knew from the tone of his voice that saying no wasn't an option. Slade waved an antenna at the weird-looking creature, who was slowly walking back across the concrete floor.

'That is our latest . . . colleague,' announced Slade grandly. 'Say hello to Juno.'

12

The monster's head jerked our way when the cockroach spoke the name. I saw then that *it* was a *she*. She speared me with a glare that made me want to run away as fast as my six legs could carry me.

'Juno comes from a long way away,' continued Slade, 'and, I mean a *long* way. See, there she was, back in her nice warm home, just resting inside a big old bunch of bananas, when suddenly—hey, what do you know?—some Human goes and chops the whole bunch down and chucks it in a crate. Next thing, they're chucking the crate into a ship, and there it sits for days and days, in the dark. And there Juno sits too. Not a clue what was going on, poor thing.' Slade's voice wasn't exactly dripping with sympathy. 'Well, no prizes for guessing what happens. The ship lands and the crate of bananas fetches up not far from here, down at the supermarket.'

The super-what? I didn't ask—I didn't want to give Slade the satisfaction—but the look on my face betrayed me. Slade seized the opportunity, addressing the insects around him.

'I forgot . . . Bug doesn't know or care about what Humans get up to. Right, Bug? He's a country boy at heart.' The cockroach smirked for the benefit of the boys, and then, as if I'd just hatched out of my egg, he explained to me nice and slowly, 'A supermarket is a place where Humans buy food and stuff. You should check one out the next time your dinner turns round and tries to eat you in that Garden of yours.

'So, anyway, some Human is there unloading bananas when out pops Juno. A bit of a shock probably. I mean, how often is it you see a scorpion round here?'

I was beginning to feel as dumb as a bedbug. A scorpion? I wasn't familiar with the name, but something about it shot a chill of fear through my shell.

Slade was watching my reaction carefully. 'Well, Juno was pretty shocked too. She ran for it, but she had no idea where to go. Everything was strange and different. For one thing, we might call this a heatwave, but she's used to much hotter weather.' The roach turned his attention to the thing he'd called the 'scorpion'.

'BIT CHILLY HERE!' he bellowed suddenly. Despite the high volume of the cockroach's shout, the scorpion didn't show any signs of understanding.

'See, the other problem,' said Slade, 'she doesn't really follow our language.' He turned to the scorpion again. 'I SAY, NO UNDERSTAND THE LINGO, EH?'

The scorpion's face was as expressive as a brick. Now that the creature was closer, I could see that it wasn't even an insect. Judging from its eight legs, it was an arachnid, but not like any I'd ever set eyes on before. Not with those immense pincers and that lethal-looking sting at the end of its tail. But still, an arachnid's an arachnid, and that makes it a deadly and ancient enemy for a lot of insects. You can count me among them.

Slade went on with the story. 'Well, she wandered around for a while, not really having much of a clue what was going on. Ended up in your neck of the woods, out in the Garden.'

A memory drifted to the surface of my mind like an air bubble rising. I remembered the look of terror on that toad's slobbery face. Something nasty lurking in the chrysanthemum bush. Now I knew what it was, I felt an unfamiliar pang of sympathy for the toad. No wonder it had looked so afraid.

'Things weren't looking great,' continued Slade, 'and they only got worse when it started to rain. Juno was trying to find some shelter up near the House, when some hedgehog stumbled upon her. Probably thought it had come across a nice tasty meal—you know, some exotic foodstuff? Well, that hedgehog was in for a surprise. There was something of a . . . disagreement, and the hedgehog came out of it the big loser.'

OK, things were falling into place. I knew now what Netta's monster was. I knew the identity of the monster in the rain.

Slade paused and looked across to a new figure that had crept into the cellar. It was Slippery Pete, the skinny grey silverfish I'd seen working the scam with Moose on fight night. He still looked as shifty as smoke, but right away I could tell that something about him was different. A new-found swagger. Pete had always been a small-timer. He'd been on the scene a long time, but he'd never played in the big leagues. Times had changed, and I soon found out why when he opened his mouth and started speaking to the scorpion.

The silverfish spoke falteringly. I couldn't follow a single word but the scorpion could. She listened carefully, and then slowly nodded her head at the tiny silverfish. I was kind of surprised that Pete had such hidden talents, but you never know with primitive insects like silverfish. They aren't like other insects— they've been around forever, far longer than most insects. They've never even had wings, and they don't go through any kind of metamorphosis. But I guess they make up for their deficiencies in other ways. Perhaps knowing the ancient tongue of the arachnids was one of these?

'See?' said Slade by my side. 'The fight ended early and Pete was on his way back to the House. Juno was still hanging around after her run-in with the hedgehog. And guess what? Pete could communicate with her. You never know with those primitive insects . . . am I right? Well, straight off old Pete saw the business opportunities the situation had to offer. He explained to Juno that he knew someone who could help her out. Help her to know who were her enemies and who were her friends in this strange new place. Maybe eventually help her find her way home . . . '

'And that someone was you?'

'Bingo! You're smarter than you look, Bug.'

'I have moments.' I checked out the scorpion again. She looked like a lean, mean killing machine. 'And in the meantime, you've got yourself a little out-of-town muscle so you can clean up and take over the other gangs in the area?'

The grinning cockroach went on grinning. 'That's just the start of it, Bug. I have big plans, and I mean BIG. We've put up with these rats long enough, so we're going to get rid of them. It'll be a doddle with Juno on our side. After that, you've gotta believe all the gangs will fall in line. We'll have ourselves an army. And then—' Another lightning flash of grin. '—who knows?'

I didn't feel the need to answer. I knew what was going on in Slade's head. He was the same as any other small-time hood, only more so.

Slippery Pete had begun to raise his voice now. The scorpion was saying something back to him, though in such a quiet whisper that I could hear nothing.

'What did she say?' demanded Slade.

'She wants to know *why*,' explained the silverfish. 'She wants to know what the rats have done to us . . . ' This was starting to get interesting.

'Tell her it's none of her business!' snapped Slade. Then he reconsidered. 'No, wait! Tell her that we have to deal with our worst enemies before we can even think about how to get her home. We can't do much planning from inside a rat's belly, can we?'

Slippery Pete began relaying this message to the scorpion, the long feelers at his tail twirling slow circles in the air. Meanwhile Slade started asking me why I was in the House.

'Couple of reasons,' I answered. 'Netta here was on the hedgehog when it ran into your new friend. The other fleas hopped ship in time. We reckon they came into the House, so they're probably on the cat upstairs. I'm reuniting her with her friends.'

While I spoke Netta stayed tucked in behind me. I could tell she was nervous around these House-insects. Smart kid. And of course, there was always the scorpion. Chances were the flea's memories had come flooding back to her at the sight of that creature. I can't imagine they were especially fond memories.

'And what's the other thing?' Slade asked me.

'There are a lot of rumours flying around the Garden about monsters . . . now I know why. There's also a bunch of insects that have gone missing. Would that have anything to do with your new friend as well?'

'Could be.' Slade shrugged as if he really didn't care. 'I think Pete took her outside this morning . . . I would guess any insect that got a glimpse of Juno would be looking for another Garden pretty fast, wouldn't you?'

'It's possible, I suppose.' Here was my chance to get at what was really on my mind. 'But what about a grasshopper, name of Velma? She wouldn't run, but she's gone missing too . . . '

The cockroach didn't miss a beat. 'You know her? Yeah, yeah, she was round here earlier on today. An hour or two ago, wasn't it, Rocky?'

The roach called Rocky responded with a razor-sharp 'Huh?'

'Forget it,' snapped Slade. 'I wouldn't want your brain to melt down. Yeah . . . I'm sure it was end of the morning. She didn't say anything about missing bugs, but she sure wanted to know what had happened to that hedgehog.'

'What did you tell her?'

Slade opened his antennae wide. 'Hey, I have nothing to hide. I told her everything I've told you. She had herself a good look at Juno, she asked a few more questions, then she hopped off out of here. You didn't see her back in the Garden?'

'I didn't see her.' I was trying to figure out the timing in my head. I guess it was possible that Velma and I had just missed each other. Perhaps she was back at Dixie's right now passing on the story to the MayDay committee? There was only one other explanation I could think of, but there wasn't really a polite way to ask if things like scorpions like to eat things like grasshoppers. If the answer was yes, I wasn't in much of a position to do anything about it.

All that was left for me to do was reunite Netta with her crewmates. Judging from the way she was huddling up against me, the little flea was more than ready.

'Well, we'd better be on our way,' I said, as casually as I could.

The cockroach nodded slowly. 'That'd be fine, Bug.'

I wasn't really asking for permission, but this wasn't the time to quibble.

'The cat's usually upstairs,' said Slade. 'There aren't any Humans around at the moment, so you'll have a clear run.'

Really? 'I'm not being suspicious, Slade, but what about all those noises from upstairs. It sure sounds like there are Humans around.'

The cockroach shook his head sadly at my ignorance. 'Bug, Bug, Bug . . . You don't know anything about life in a House, do you? There are noises all the time—water pipes, stuff like that. It doesn't mean there's anyone in. Just turn right after you get out of the Cellar, then head up the other stairs. You can't go wrong. Trust me. '

Generally I would trust Slade about as far as I'd trust a tarantula, but there wasn't much I could do about it now.

'Come on, Netta,' I said to the little flea. She bounded up onto my back eagerly.

'It's been nice,' said Slade, still playing the amiable crime lord. 'Don't be such a stranger in future.'

We started towards the stairs that led up and out of the Cellar, when Moose came lumbering up. The big stag beetle seemed nervous addressing Slade.

'Boss, I could escort them upstairs . . . You know, keep an eye on 'em or something?' In his way, I suppose Moose was trying to make it up to me for saving his life back at the club. It was kinda touching.

But even before Slade could respond, Slippery Pete was shouting across the floor. 'Hey, Moose,' snapped the silverfish. 'Engage brain before operating mandibles, willya? Better yet, let me do the thinking for ya. For now, just stay put. Bug's a big boy. He can look after himself.'

'Yeah,' mumbled the stag beetle. 'I guess so, Pete.'

By the time we reached the stairs, Slade had already moved on to more important matters. He was planning the next stage of his war against the rats. I looked back one last time. At this distance it was hard to make out the smaller bugs, but I could see the giant scorpion well enough. She sat in silence, not understanding a word, while all around her insects discussed the many ways in which she could do their killing for them.

13

Netta and I crawled through the crack under the Cellar door. Suddenly we were back in a world of sunlight, though we were still inside the House.

I knew Netta had a lot on her mind. I guessed it was thoughts of the scorpion, but the flea was turning out to be tougher than I'd imagined. When she spoke up at last, she sounded more angry than afraid.

'I don't think I like your friends very much,' she said.

I laughed. 'Not everyone can judge characters so well,' I told her. 'You'll go a long way, kid.'

I looked around trying to get my bearings in this weird environment. Human furniture towered around us like a nightmare forest. I'd visited the Cellar once before—a long time ago—but this was my first time in the upstairs part of the House. Maybe I should have been taking in the sights, but this was no time for tourism. I just wanted to get this job over and done with, and then get the heck out of there.

'Slade said to go right, didn't he?' I turned in that direction. I didn't get far before I realized that Netta had hopped off onto the floor.

'What's the matter?'

The little flea wasn't budging. 'That's the wrong way,' she said. 'I know it is.' Her voice trembled, but there was steel in it. In her eyes I glimpsed the determination I had seen back at the rosebush.

'Why?'

'The cat's this way,' insisted the flea, indicating the opposite direction. 'I can *smell* it.'

I weighed up the alternatives. On the one hand was the nose for blood of a hungry flea. On the other hand was the advice of Slade, a cockroach I knew only too well from way back when. It wasn't a hard choice.

'Lead the way,' I said.

We set off down a long narrow room. Walking on the concrete in the cellar had been bad enough, but this stuff was the worst—the whole floor was covered with some springy synthetic fabric. Carpet, they call it. It was harder than pushing your way through the thickest grass.

But Netta had been right. We came to a doorway at the end of the thin room and there it was, sleeping peacefully. The cat.

When Netta caught sight of it, she couldn't stop herself from leaping in excitement. Every nerve in her body must have been screaming at her to get stuck in and start feeding. I knew the kid was starving, but she was polite too. She took the time to turn to me.

'Gee, Bug, I don't know what I'd have done without you. I—'

This was sounding like the start of something mushy. Not my style, so I cut in fast.

'Hey, kid, I'm picking up a paycheque for this, remember?' I nodded towards the slumbering mammal. 'Go get yourself something to eat.'

Netta grinned a big old blood-suckin' grin. Then she

leapt up right at the sleeping animal, spinning her body in a typical display of midair acrobatics. She landed on the cat's back leg and moments later I saw a little cluster of fleas appear on the fur in the same area. I could hear all these little yippees of excitement as Netta was reunited with her friends. Cute.

Life isn't usually so simple and I gave myself two seconds to enjoy the moment. But then it was time to get out of here and fast. I looked around quickly, saw that there was no way to the outside from this room. I would have to head back the way I had just come. When I got to the doorway, I looked back once, just in time to see the sleeping cat swishing its tail from side to side. I knew Netta must be tucking in. Good for her. A lot of insects look down on parasites, but the way I figure it, everyone's got to make a living one way or another. Maybe it wasn't quite so nice for the cat, but then again what did one more passenger matter?

I was out in that long thin room now and moving pretty fast. I'd had enough of being in this House. It made me nervous, and when I get nervous I can't think straight. It was time to get home and get things sorted in my mind. I had plenty to tell the MayDay Committee, but I knew I didn't have all the answers yet. There was something still troubling me, something hiding in the back of my mind, just waiting for me to coax it out. But what?

I had returned Netta to her crewmates, and I had found out the identity of the killer in the rain. My job seemed to be done. So what was wrong? I couldn't quite put an antenna on it. Perhaps it was Slade's explanation for why all those insects had suddenly gone missing from the Garden. Did it make sense that so many would have fled after seeing Juno? As I recalled the horrific sight of the giant scorpion, I told myself that it was certainly a possibility.

And yet . . . Perhaps there was another explanation, but it wasn't one I wanted to think about too much. Scorpions have to eat, don't they? Perhaps the missing insects had become scorpion food.

And what about Velma? There was no way *she* would have fled. Again, Slade's explanation was possible—that we had simply missed each other while Velma left the House and I entered it. And yet, and yet . . .

These were the thoughts buzzing around my brain, and the buzzing got so loud that I didn't hear the usual warning signals around me. Like some dumb novice fresh out of metamorphosis, I wandered right into danger. The first clue I got was when a terrible noise tore through the air.

I looked up at the Human which was looking down at me. Its mouth was open wide and that weird noise was still coming from it, like 'EEEK!' This was bad news. I was out in the open here. There was no furniture to scurry under. There was no way to dig to safety. I pelted for the skirting board.

Too late. The Woman was moving now, an immense, blurred shape looming above me. Suddenly there were two gigantic feet in front of me, and then, just as suddenly, there was only one. I knew what was coming.

Quite a few insects have encountered the Boot from Above, but not many have lived to tell their grandlarvae about it. A wedge of darkness appeared above me—the bottom of the Woman's shoe. The shape got bigger and bigger until I could see nothing else.

There was no point in running further—you can't outrun the Boot. I tucked my legs in under my shell as fast as I could. I was just in time. An instant later everything was darkness and an enormous weight was pressing down on me. I was under the Boot.

The pressure was terrible, but I was lucky. If I'd been on concrete or wood or even grass, I'd have been smashed as flat as a leaf, no doubt about it. What saved me was this carpet stuff. It was so thick and springy, and when the Boot descended, it just pressed me down further into the carpet. You can say what you like about Humans, but I won't hear a bad word said about carpet.

My shell was taking the pressure, but that didn't mean I was having a blast down there. If I ever got out of this alive, I was going to have a killer of a headache.

Suddenly the pressure was gone and I could see again. The Woman had pulled her Boot back. I knew I would have to time this just right. I stayed perfectly still and let it examine the damage. Just a moment more and then . . . NOW. I was up and running towards the skirting board again.

The Human let out another of those screaming noises. I tried not to let it put me off my stride. I was moving it some—out-and-out fear can do wonders for your sprinting ability.

I made it to the skirting board, but the Woman wasn't done yet. It—no, wait, it was the female of the species—*she* realized that she couldn't stamp a foot on me now because the wall was in the way, but she was pulling off one of her Boots. She gripped it in one hand like a weapon and began hammering at me.

The noise as the Boot struck the wooden skirting board was deafening, but there was more noise than danger. The Boot was too thick to get right into the corner where floor and wall met. That was my safety zone and I stayed inside it, scurrying along the edge of the wall as fast as I could.

Suddenly the floor was rumbling with the sound of giant footsteps. Had the Human given up? Was I in the clear?

Yeah, right . . . and all spiders are fly-lovin' vegetarians.

I looked back, and the Woman was standing at another door down the other end of the long, thin room. She was pulling out something big, something which she began dragging towards me. It had a sort of box at one end and what looked like a huge metal snake at the other. The Woman used one foot to push something on the box end, and the thing began to roar.

I've since learned what they're called. Ever heard of a vacuum cleaner?

14

It was a fearsome weapon all right.

The Woman stomped towards me, pushing the snaky bit forward and holding the mouth part against the carpet. The din was terrible. And here's the thing—that machine was sucking everything up off the carpet. All the dirt, all the crumbs, all the bits of fluff. Everything just shot right up into the blackness of that dreadful slot.

I tried to run faster but I was already at top speed. I knew I wouldn't be able to hold on once that nightmare machine reached me. But my luck was in—I reached a patch where the carpet was worn. There was a hole just big enough for me to push my way through.

That's what I did, and moments later I was in total darkness. I stopped and caught my breath. Above me the carpet, below me the wooden floorboards, and all around me the din of the vacuum cleaner. I began to shove my way forward. It was hard going and I wasn't making very good progress, but I kept on, mainly because there was nothing else I could do.

Suddenly the darkness around me vanished. The carpet was gone. The Woman was above me, bending down and folding back the edge of the carpet with one giant hand. In her other hand she held the vacuum. I was exposed again. The Woman must have realized what I'd done and she wasn't going to be outsmarted by a beetle.

The Woman was fiddling with the end of the vacuum cleaner now. She was pulling off the wide mouthpart so that the tube ended in a smaller, round hole. That meant that she could get the thing right into the corner along the wall. I looked across the expanse of floorboard to where the carpet began again. There was no way I could make it in time.

The vacuum cleaner mouth was closing down on me from above. Already I could feel its incredible force almost lifting me off my feet. I tried to tighten my grip on the grainy wood below. I knew it wouldn't do me much good. It would be impossible to hold on, to resist the power of that jet stream.

Unless . . .

I let go. Before the metal pipe closed around me, I hopped up into the air, aiming myself for the machine itself. At the same time I opened my wings. Once I was off the ground I could feel the power of the machine. I was moving pretty fast. Any second now I would disappear into the blackness of that tube.

I beat my wings as hard as I could. It was like swimming against a raging current. The force of the air rushing around my wings almost slammed them back into my shell, but I managed to keep them open long enough. One big beat was all it took. The hole of the vacuum cleaner tube was right ahead of me, but I just managed to flip myself out of the jet of air sucking me upwards. It was the kind of aerial move that owes a lot to fleas.

I didn't even need to fly the rest of the way. Physics did the job for me, and I flipped across the hallway and landed on the wall opposite. I almost bounced right off it, but the wallpaper had enough of a bumpy pattern for me to gain a foothold and keep it.

I didn't know if the Woman had noticed that I'd escaped the vacuum cleaner of Death, but I wasn't going to take any chances. There was a picture frame right above me. I scuttled upwards and slipped behind it.

I was in cool darkness again. I listened to the enraged sound of the vacuum for a few minutes more, then it clicked off. There was the sound of footsteps clumping away. Had the Human really gone or was she bluffing me? I didn't think Humans were smart enough to play that old trick, but you never know. I stayed put. I wasn't dumb.

It gave me time to think things over some more. So . . . Slade had been wrong about there being no Humans around up here. My first question was—how wrong? Was the Woman alone, or were there other Humans I was in danger of running into?

The second question was even more troubling—*why* had Slade been wrong? Was he simply mistaken, or had the cockroach known what was waiting for Netta and me upstairs?

I stayed put a few minutes more. When I was convinced that the Woman had really, definitely gone, I crawled out from behind the picture frame. I figured that the Human would still be on the ground floor somewhere, so I continued upwards, climbing up the wall to the top floor of the House. The day was still hot, even in late afternoon, and I reckoned there *had* to be an open window up there. I'd make my escape that way.

When I was high enough up the wall, I switched from vertical to horizontal, hopping across to the landing floor. It didn't take long to find what I was looking for. I struck gold at the first doorway. I could feel a gentle breeze blowing out onto the landing. Sure enough, the window was partly open in there. A way out! I could almost taste the honeydew at Dixie's already.

And that's when Fate whacked me in the head with another sucker punch.

I'd like to tell you that it was my phenomenal powers of deductive reasoning that led me to the Boy's room. It wasn't. I'd like to tell you that it was my uncanny intuition, one I had honed and perfected over a long and varied career as a detective. It wasn't that either.

It was dumb old luck that had brought me upstairs, and now it was dumb old luck that let me hear, moments before I made my exit, a familiar high-pitched noise. It was coming from somewhere further along the landing. The noise was muffled, but I could tell that it was a grasshopper's song. It was giving the universal insect-in-distress call. Velma!

I took one last look at the open window and the greenery of the Garden beyond. The distress call sounded again, and once I was back out on the landing I could tell which room it was coming from. I wasted no time. I charged into the room. More of that furniture stuff loomed over me. I paused in the doorway, waiting for the signal to sound one more time. When it did, I was able to pinpoint where it was coming from—somewhere on top of the table in the corner. I ran further into the room and that's when my detective instincts kicked in— better late than never, I guess. What they were telling me was that something wasn't quite right in this place. I just couldn't see what it was.

That soon changed when I crawled up the table leg. Once I was up on the top, I noticed something—an insect's leg. It was lying on a clean white surface. I couldn't say what kind of insect it belonged to. That's because the leg was no longer attached to a body. It looked kinda sad lying there without its five buddies.

A little further along was a thorax. It too was neatly detached from the rest of its body. Nice. Then I spotted someone I recognized. It was the tiger beetle larva, the one who'd tried to dine on Netta only this morning. Of course, he'd changed some. Having your head removed will do that to a bug.

'You were right, pal,' I murmured. 'You said we'd meet again.' The bodyless head wasn't saying anything.

There were some other bits 'n' pieces lying around, but I'll spare the graphic description, in case you're thinking of eating anything in the next twenty-four hours.

The words of that screwball death watch beetle came back to me—'This is Death's house,' he had said. Maybe it *was*. Maybe this was Death's bedroom right here? Perhaps I should start rapping my head against the wooden table?

Things got worse when I went further along the table. There was a flat tray and inside it were several insects. They weren't moving too much, if you get my meaning. Each one was held neatly in place with a shiny metal pin.

I couldn't handle more of this. I charged along the table top, scurrying round a stack of books. Down at the far end, several glass jars were neatly lined up. Inside each one was an insect. These ones were a little more animated than the poor saps in the tray—that is to say, at least these were alive—but they weren't exactly jumping for joy. They all eyed me glumly from their glass prisons.

I wasn't sure, but I thought I recognized the shield bug in the jar on the left. There was an alder fly and a ground beetle too, but it was the jar in the middle that I rushed towards.

I'd seen Velma looking happier. You couldn't really blame her. She had stopped rubbing her wings together to make the call for help now. When she saw me, the grasshopper jumped up against the smooth insides of the jar. Her front legs began tapping frantically on the glass. I knew she was trying to tell me something, but what?

'I can't hear you!' I shouted as loud as I could. 'What?'

As I neared the jar, I could just about hear her voice, but not what she was shouting. I ran on towards her. By the time I realized that the breeze in the room had changed direction, it was too late. That was a shame— see, the breeze had altered because something was moving in the room. Something big.

There wasn't time to open my wing casing and fly away. There wasn't time to scurry off. One moment I was charging headlong towards Velma. The next moment I was running smack into an invisible wall. WHAM!

Working on instinct and nothing else, I wheeled around and pelted in the opposite direction. WHAM! The wall was there too. It was everywhere. I was trapped in a see-through prison, just as Velma was. A drinking glass had been placed upside-down over me.

I could see the massive bulk of the Human in the room. From where I was, I couldn't really make out its giant, fleshy features, but something told me this wasn't the Woman from downstairs.

Things were moving quickly. Suddenly a sheet of paper was shoved underneath the glass. Then the whole thing—the glass, the paper, and yours truly, Bug Muldoon—was being lifted into the air. There was a pause of a few seconds, and then the paper beneath my feet was whipped away and I was tumbling down.

I had been emptied into Velma's jar. The grasshopper had to do a nifty sidestep to avoiding having me land on her head. I struggled to my feet and looked up, just in time to see the top of the jar twisting shut. It was pierced with several air holes, but nothing big enough to squeeze through.

I looked at my good friend Velma. 'Fancy seeing you here,' I said. 'Let me guess what you were trying to tell me just now.'

Velma wasn't in the mood for guessing games. 'I was saying, "Behind you".'

'Ah.'

15

Suddenly five enormous pink fingers wrapped themselves around the jar and we were being lifted into the air. A vast human eye drew level with us. I never knew how unnerving it is to be watched by an eyeball that's as big as you are.

'It's the Boy,' muttered Velma bitterly.

Velma's species of grasshopper is one that has a special kind of defence. When they're attacked, they can spit out this dark red foam. It isn't all that poisonous, but it's acidic enough to scare off a lot of enemies.

'If you're squeamish,' she said to me now, 'look away.'

'I'll get by.'

I watched as Velma began to produce this discharge. She spat the stuff onto the side of the jar. If the glass wall hadn't been in the way, the stuff would have gone right in the Boy's eye. It didn't do us any good, but I appreciated the symbolism of the gesture.

I guess the Boy *didn't*. Those immense fingers stayed wrapped around the jar, but the eyeball was gone. The lid at the top of the jar began to slowly turn open. I didn't know what the Boy had in mind, but it probably wasn't a lively inter-species discussion. I thought again about those poor dead bugs all lined up in a row and held in place by giant pins. Call me a non-conformist if you like, but I wasn't keen to take my place in the line-up. I'm kinda squeamish when it comes to pins, especially when I think some Human is going to fix my lifeless body to a tray with one.

But then suddenly there was a movement in the room, a streak of orange on the floor below us. I couldn't make out much. The thing, whatever it was, was smaller than a Human—though still much, much bigger than any insect. The top of our lid was tightened back up and then we were flying through the air. The Boy had thrown the jar aside! Tumbling against each other, Velma and I got ready for the impact.

It didn't come. The jar landed on something soft. I realized that it was near the foot of that thing Humans like to sleep on, the bed. The Boy's nocturnal nesting material—the bedding—was heaped up in a pile and our jar had settled into a fold so we were set almost vertical. This position gave us a better view of the room. We could see now what the streak of orange was—a cat, the same one that I had returned Netta to.

The Boy looked angry. It was bending down and scooping the cat up with two hands. I wasn't too sure why—must have been one of those territorial things mammals get so worked up about. Whatever, the smaller animal let out a huffy miaow we could hear right through our glass prison.

We watched as the Boy marched the protesting cat out of the room, closing the door behind it with one vast foot. We went on watching the door, but it didn't open again. We were alone for now.

I looked at Velma and she looked right back at me.

'So . . . who's footing the bill for this little rescue expedition, Bug?' she asked.

That hurt. 'This one's a freebie,' I said. 'I guess I just got curious.'

Velma laughed. She was too classy to say how I *was* concerned after all or anything corny like that. But with that short laugh I got the feeling that Velma and I had deepened our friendship. It was one of those touching moments you sometimes hear about, but as usual there was no time to enjoy it. We had to get down to business.

'OK, would you like to tell me your story first?' said the grasshopper.

'It's a long one,' I said. 'We'd be better off spending our time trying to get out of this place.' As I spoke, I started trying to climb up the glass sides of our prison. The jar was no longer completely upright and I thought I might be able to make it. No dice. My feet slipped immediately.

Velma watched me struggle for a bit before she said, 'I hate to burst your bubble, Bug, but we aren't going anywhere. Trust me—I've spent ages trying. Even if you could make it to the top—which you can't—that lid is screwed on tight. The holes are too small. We'd never get out. Not without help.'

I slumped down. It was true. 'OK,' I said. 'But I'd hate to spoil the surprise. Why don't you go ahead and tell me what happened to you first?'

Velma's a professional reporter, and she did a good job of keeping it short and to the point, but not missing out any essential information. Here's how she told it:

Velma *had* actually come around the House first thing in the morning. She'd soon run into a roach, a member of Slade's gang, and had asked him a bunch of questions. She didn't get many answers.

'He didn't mention something called a scorpion?' I asked.

'A what? No.'

'Must have slipped his mind, I guess. And you weren't

taken to meet a roach called Slade? Ambitious guy—
grins a lot.'

'No. Why?'

'I'm just trying to work out why I was lied to earlier on
today,' I said.

Velma went on. She hadn't been too impressed with the
roach's answers. Like any top-notch reporter, she knew a
cover-up when she heard one. She was just looking for a
way into the House to do some investigating of her own,
when along came the Boy.

'The one you were writing a feature on?'

'The same one.'

Well, Velma didn't pay much attention to the kid. Her
mind was on other things. It turned out to be a bad
mistake, because moments later the Boy had caught her
in a glass jar. Before she knew it she was sitting in the jar
in this room, along with all the other insects trapped on
Death Row.

'That's a cute name. Why Death Row?' I asked.

Velma shook her head in disgust. 'This Boy . . . it's not
like any Human I've watched before. It doesn't just kill
insects that get in its way. It's *methodical*. It's as if it's
studying the bugs it kills. You wouldn't believe what it's
been doing.'

'I saw some of the evidence on the table top,' I said
grimly. I'd always heard rumours that there were some
Humans who would kill an insect just for the heck of it.
Freaky young Humans who pulled the legs off spiders,
stuff like that. I'd never believed the rumours—I mean,
why would any species act that way? What purpose could
it serve? Well, I was a believer now, and how.

I thought about everything Velma had told me. Then I
saw the expectant look on the grasshopper's face. It was
my turn to talk. I tried to cover everything—how Netta
and I had gone to the Professor, the hypnosis session and

our eventful dash back to the Garden. I explained about the confrontation in the Cellar, and I did my best to describe the scorpion. I relayed all the lies Slade had told about seeing Velma earlier that day.

'What I'm not clear about is *why* he would lie,' I added. We talked about the case some more, but pretty soon we found ourselves up against a wall as impenetrable as the one that held us prisoner. The silences became more and more frequent.

When she spoke again, I expected Velma to ask me more about Juno, but she surprised me by focusing on something completely different.

'So tell me . . . What's the deal with you and this Slade?' asked the grasshopper. 'How far back do you two go?'

I thought for a moment. I don't go blabbing too much about my old life. To be honest, I'm not so proud of it. But, I figured, hey, Velma was a good friend, and what the heck? The way things were shaping up, this might be our last conversation.

But where to begin? 'Well . . . I was a pretty good larva, I suppose. Never got into trouble, at least. But after metamorphosis I kinda fell in with a bad crowd. Nothing too serious at first. You know, we were just dumb young bugs, up to no good. But then Slade came along . . . '

'And things got a little more serious, right?'

I smiled. 'You got it. Are you a reporter or something? Yeah, he was a cockroach with big plans, and he had the smarts to get other bugs to help out too.'

'What, even you, Mr Independent Private Eye?'

I didn't join in with Velma's smile. 'Me and Slade were pretty tight buddies . . . It wasn't as if I didn't have plans too.' I paused, thinking about the old days. There was a tale or two I could tell Velma, but I decided to stick to the essentials. 'Well, back then there was a big bee hive not too far away. Slade and I kept joking about how much all that honey must be worth and how we and a few of the boys should pull a robbery on the hive. We kept on talking and joking, only soon the jokes had run out, and we were still talking. It started to make more and more sense. We were going to do it.'

Velma couldn't hide her amazement. 'You planned a hive robbery?'

'We did. It was a lot of work, too. Slade was good on the big picture—he's a big picture kinda guy—but he didn't care too much about the little details. That was my area. See, I reckoned we had to plan everything down to the tiniest detail. I was a real stickler. I made sure the whole gang saw things my way, too, even when they didn't really want to be bothered.'

'I can picture it now,' said Velma.

'Yeah, it was back then that I got my nickname.'

Velma seemed more interested in this than in anything I'd said so far that afternoon. 'You mean . . . ?'

I nodded. 'It got so I was asking Slade and the others so many questions, and he told me to get off his back and stop bugging him. Said I should be called "Bug" Muldoon. The other guys fixed on to it and the name stuck.'

I could see a question making its way to Velma's mouth, but I went on with the story.

'Well, soon enough the day of the big hive job came around. I won't go into it blow-by-blow. All you need to know is, the hold-up started out pretty smoothly. We'd planned it well and everyone did their job. No one in the hive was dumb enough to be a hero just for the sake of a load of honey, and that meant no bees were getting hurt, which was how I'd said it had to be. It was looking like we'd be out of there and home free. But then our lookout guy starts shouting.'

'Who was the lookout?'

'Silverfish, name of Pete.'

'The same bug who was working that scam at Dixie's on fight night?' You can't get much past Velma.

I nodded. 'That's the creep. So Slippery Pete, he starts shouting about how he can see a patrol of ants coming along. And that's when all hell breaks loose. The whole gang of us charge out and we see the ants are almost here. They're not even soldiers, they're just some hicks driving a herd of greenflies back from their feed. If we'd kept our heads, we could have dealt with the situation and no one would have been hurt. But we didn't keep our heads. We just put them down and ran, and that's when I hit the greenfly. Ran right into it, flattened the little thing.

'All of the other guys were hightailing it out of there at top speed. And Slade, he was ahead of all of them. I knew he'd seen the greenfly hit the dust, but he didn't care whether it was hurt or not. Not Slade. He just flew out of there. Looking out for Number One, same as usual.'

'But you stayed, huh, Bug?'

'I stayed. I stayed until the greenfly came to and asked what was going on. By that time there was a whole bunch of angry bees around me, and a whole bunch of soldier ants on their way.' I chuckled at the memory. It wasn't all that funny, but sometimes chuckling is all you can do about the mistakes that litter your past. 'And that was the end of my life of crime. I served my prison time over at the rock garden. It wasn't a laugh a minute, but I kept my antennae clean, and I did a lot of thinking. On my first day back on the outside, I applied for my private detective licence.'

'That's a touching story,' said Velma, doing a pretty good job of not sounding too touched. 'But you didn't mention one thing. If "Bug" is just your nickname, then what's your real name?'

I was about to tell her, I swear I was. I mean, what's in a name? What would it matter if Velma became the first bug in ages to learn my real name? But suddenly there were more important topics of conversation. My eye caught sight of something zipping past the open window. Make that *someone*. He turned round and zipped by again. I knew that flight pattern anywhere.

'What is it?' asked Velma.

'It's a housefly, and I'm pretty certain I know who. It's Jake!'

16

Shaky Jake often came up near the House on his constant search for a fix of sugar, though he no longer ventured inside. A nasty experience with a rolled-up newspaper had cured him of that. This time I guessed he was on a different mission. The fly would be looking for Netta. I knew Jake would feel terrible about letting me down like that.

I tried shouting to our friend as loudly as I could. It was no good. The holes punched into the lid of the jar were too small. There was no way anything outside the window could hear me.

But Velma had been thinking about this. 'Step back,' she told me. 'This is *my* line of work. I should stand a better chance now the jar is nearer the window.'

Once she had enough room, the grasshopper opened her wings. She began to rub one wing's scraper across the ridge on the other wing again. The high-pitched noise was deafening inside that jar. I watched the window eagerly. If he could hear it, then Jake would be able to recognize Velma's distress call. The only thing was— could he hear it?

Seconds crept by. Velma went on scraping and nothing flew through the window. He mustn't have heard us. Disappointment flowered in my heart like a sprig of poison ivy.

But then suddenly a heroic black shape zipped into view. Jake! He hesitated at the window, and then flew inside, zigzagging across the room while he found his bearings. He spotted us and came in for a landing on the bed, right next to the jar.

He had to come right up to the glass for us to hear him, and even then he had to yell as loudly as he could. 'V-V-Velma? Bug!' Shaky Jake didn't seem to have the shakes so badly now. I remembered what Netta had said about him finding a boiled sweet. 'I was l-looking for the f-f-flea. She g-got away, Bug. I'm s-s-s—'

'Apology accepted!' I yelled. 'Netta's fine. We've got other things on our mind now . . . '

Jake stared at our glass prison. 'What's going o-on?'

'We're taking a vacation,' I shouted back. 'The weather's nice but the room service stinks. We want out of here.'

'I don't think I c-c-c-can do m-much to help,' said the fly. 'This jar is too b-b-big.'

Velma cut in. 'Just fly and get help outside, Jake.'

'As many bugs as you can find,' I added. 'This kid's a nutball.'

There's an old earthworm saying: *Speak of the magpie and down he'll fly.* The idea is, learn to keep your big fat mandibles shut. That's what I was wishing I'd done, because right then there was the rumble of footsteps. The massive door swung open and the Boy stepped back into the room.

'Go, Jake! Now!' I yelled.

Jake took to the air, just like any housefly would have done in the same situation. If he'd flown straight for the open window, he'd have made it too.

The problem was, Shaky Jake didn't know what we were dealing with here. This wasn't your ordinary type of Human. OK, it's not as if lots of Humans haven't stepped on one or two bugs—one or two thousand, even. But not many of them go out of their way to catch insects, take them home and *then* set about killing them.

It wasn't done in self-defence. It wasn't done for food. As far as I could tell, it was just for kicks, nothing more.

In my book, that's weird.

But there was something else about the Boy. Unlike most of the clumsy clodhoppers in its species, this kid was fast. It slipped into the room quickly and quietly. The door closed behind it. While Jake was banking left and looping round the perimeter of the room at a steady cruise, the Boy strode across the floor and shoved the window shut—now there was no way out. Then it swept something up from the table top.

I could see instantly that what it held in its hand was a deadly weapon. I now know what that weapon is called—'comic'. The name alone is enough to send chills through any winged insect. The Boy held the weapon up alongside its fleshy, human head and planted itself stock-still in the middle of the room. It didn't flail its arms or run around and shout like a lot of Humans would. It just stood there. Only its eyes moved. They followed Jake's flight path around the room.

There was nothing for Velma and me to do but watch. Jake was holding a standard zigzag evasive pattern. He was good, but I didn't know if he was good enough. It was when he flew over the table top that Jake made his first mistake. He was cruising low and he went right over the tray of dead and pinned insects. I knew what kind of a shock the sight of that thing could give a bug, and straight-away Jake's flight pattern was all over the place.

His buzzing became erratic, and I could sense the fly's confusion and panic.

The Boy didn't miss the opportunity. It sprang forward, its massive arm swished through the air. Such sudden movement from total stillness made me think of praying mantises. It wasn't a nice thought.

The comic didn't land a clean hit, but it did strike Jake a glancing blow. The fly's buzz stuttered and he spiralled towards the floor. Was Shaky Jake out for the count? No! At the last moment he pulled out of the spin.

'Go higher!' Velma was yelling. I don't know if Jake heard her, maybe he figured it out for himself. Either way, the housefly did go high, flying up out of the Boy's deadly range. Jake landed on the ceiling and sat upside down a moment. I knew he was thinking what to do next.

Only the Boy didn't give him time to think. It wouldn't let up. It was grabbing something else now, holding it in one hand and shaking it violently. It reached up as high as it could and pointed the object at Jake. This looked bad. The Boy pressed a button on the top of the thing in its hand. *FFFSSSHHHHTT!* A jet of something burst out with a hiss that sounded like a garden snake with attitude.

Jake was in the air again, but not fast enough. The spray caught him head on. His buzz stuttered again, and this time it went on stuttering. Shaky Jake was tougher than a lot of bugs might have guessed. I don't know how he did it, but he didn't drop. Jake maintained some kind of slow and ragged flight pattern for a few more seconds, and then he lost it altogether.

He wobbled towards the window. There was no use wondering why, he wasn't thinking straight. Whatever was in that spray had really hit him hard. No one could take punishment like that. The fly flew, BANG! straight into the glass.

At last Jake fell. He landed on his back, all six legs pointing upwards and kicking like crazy. Back when I was a larva, we used to laugh and call that position things like the Dance of Death and The Terminal Shuffle. I wasn't laughing now.

I looked over at our overgrown enemy. I felt a surge of hatred and I knew I was powerless to act on it. The muscles on the Boy's face were pulling back so you could see its enormous white teeth. I've heard that's what passes for a smile with some mammals.

It took the Human no more than a couple of vast steps to cross the room to the table. It picked something up with one giant five-fingered hand and turned back towards the window. As the Human moved towards the stricken fly, sunlight glinted on the object in its hand.

A knife.

17

The only thing that could save Jake was a miracle, and you don't get many of those in my neighbourhood. But sometimes, Luck tosses you a free lunch. The Boy was almost upon Jake, when a noise rang out from downstairs in the House. It was something called the telephone. (It's sort of like the ants' system of communicating via chemicals, I think—only not so sophisticated, of course. I guess you'd have to talk to the Professor if you want to know more.)

The boy hesitated and we all listened to the faint sound of the Woman's voice downstairs. But then our enemy turned its attention back to the window ledge where Jake's legs were still twitching away. This was it, the noise from downstairs had only bought our friend a few seconds extra, and now . . .

Suddenly the Woman's voice grew louder. Judging from the Boy's reaction, the Woman was calling to it. At any rate, the Boy opened its mouth and shouted something in response. Then it put down the blade and stomped out of the room.

'Take your time about coming back,' I murmured.

'Don't kid yourself,' said Velma grimly. 'It'll be back.'

On the window ledge, the frantic kicking of Jake's legs had slowed and then stopped. Was that it? Had our friend Shaky Jake really danced the Terminal Shuffle?

Either way, there was nothing we could do about it. The Boy would be back soon enough—it had too much unfinished business up here—and then what would stop Velma and me from joining Jake in that undignified dance of the dead?

But that's when Luck provided the dessert to go with our free lunch. The Boy had not fully closed the door behind it this time, and moments later another mammal poked its head around. We'd seen that face before. It was the cat, back for another try. You had to hand it to that cat—it scored top points for persistence.

I don't know much about cats other than that they're dumb and they're entirely motivated by the search for personal comfort. This one must have been looking for a particularly cushy spot. With the Boy out of the way, the cat dashed into the room right towards the bed. As it got closer it disappeared from view for a moment, but then suddenly it was springing right up onto the bed. It chose a spot at the other end and began turning and turning in an attempt to get its position just so.

I watched the cat and tried to guess what was going on in the recesses of its small, mammalian brain. As far as I could tell, nothing apart from an overriding inner drive to get as comfy as possible. Finally it seemed to find a position that was satisfactory. Before long its eyes were just slits and its breathing slowed way down. Only its tail lazily flicked back and forth.

'What are you staring at that thing for?' asked Velma. 'I don't think we'll get much help there. From what I hear, cats are dumber than humans.'

But I wasn't staring at the cat. I was staring at something *on* the cat. On one of its ears, to be precise, where the creature's fur was much shorter. I could just make out a tiny black dot. Maybe it was wishful thinking, but I thought I knew who that little black dot was.

Netta!

Velma wasn't overjoyed. 'OK,' the grasshopper said, 'so the flea is on the cat. I don't get it. What good can a parasite do us?'

I wasn't sure myself. I hadn't known Netta for long, but I knew there was more to the flea than even she realized herself. She had real courage. Smarts, too. I had seen it on the rosebush, when we were facing those robber flies. I had seen it outside the House too. If only Netta could dig deep and discover those qualities inside her again. I found myself willing for it to happen, as if that might actually *make* it happen. (When you get desperate enough, you start acting like a little larva again, I suppose.)

But then the cat sat suddenly upright. Its back leg began scratching furiously at one ear. I just had time to glimpse a knot of fleas spring to safety away from their ship's claws. Then the cat turned around and settled back down into its favourite snooze position.

Seconds crawled by like overfed caterpillars. 'OK, OK, Netta, it's time, come on now,' I muttered underneath my breath.

Sure enough, the cluster of tiny dots reappeared on the cat's ear. Moments later, the cat let out an angry miaow and jerked up again, shaking its head. It tried to scratch itself with a rear leg again, but it didn't seem to be having too much luck.

It rolled onto its back, rubbing its head against the bedding as it did so. The move brought it a little bit closer to our end of the bed. A tiny bud of hope nudged into my mind and I prayed that the wintry cold of reality would not kill it off.

I felt a tap on my side. It was Velma. 'What's going on?' she whispered. Velma is one smart insect, but even the grasshopper couldn't figure out what this was all about.

'I can't be sure,' I answered, 'but here's what I *hope* Netta's doing. See, usually fleas just go wherever their host animal takes them, right? No responsibility. Well, I *think* Netta and her friends are trying to change all that. They're working out a way of steering the ship.'

'And how can a bunch of fleas do *that*?'

I kept my eyes on the cat. Seconds after it had settled back down, it let out another angry miaow. Then it rolled back the way it had come from, but that only seemed to make things worse. It wriggled some more, rolling closer to our jar again, then stopped.

'It's your basic system of rewards and punishments,' I said, hoping I was right. 'They give it a bit of a bite to get the ship moving. Then whenever it moves in the wrong direction, it gets a bunch more itchy bites. But when it moves in the right direction, the reward is no bites. Even something as thick as a cat should figure out what to do.'

'But will it work?'

'Hard to say. They can't steer the ship with any accuracy, but they might just be able to get it close enough to our jar.'

Even as I spoke, the cat was moving again, arching its back against the bedding as it edged closer. Velma and I watched in silence. Every time the cat made a move in the wrong direction, we could see a flurry of activity from the fleas and then the cat was back on track. It was working, but it was taking a long, long time. The only problem was, time was no pal of ours. How long before the Human Boy returned?

I tried to push such worries from my mind. I focused my whole attention on the cat's unsteady progress down the bed. The minutes stretched like the twilight shadows around us, but gradually the animal came closer and closer.

Our jar was filled with the sound of urgent chanting—'Come on, come on, come on.' I realized it was coming from me.

The cat was close enough now that, every time it moved, our jar nearly rolled into the indentation the heavy mammal made in the bedding. Nearly, but not quite. Velma and I both tried pushing on the glass to see if that would help. It didn't.

But Netta didn't give up. The cat's unwilling progress down the bed continued and at last its body was right next to the jar we were trapped in. It was so close we could look down and make out the skin beneath the thick jungle of its fur.

'What now?' asked Velma. 'The grand finale?'

'I reckon so.'

Before it happened, I saw something move through the mammal's fur. She was close enough now for me to recognize. It was Netta, but there was something different about the young flea now. At first I couldn't put my antenna on it, but then I realized. This was no longer the bewildered flea I had shepherded back to her friends and crew. She had taken control of the situation. She had assumed responsibility and actually steered the host animal. Netta had grown up.

She flashed a grin our way. That was the last I saw of her, and then she was pushing her way deeper into the undergrowth of hair and she was gone.

'Get ready,' I said to Velma. 'Here it comes.'

Every flea in the crew must have bitten at the same moment, because the cat leapt up. The timing was perfect and our luck was in. At long last the jar rolled down into the indentation left by the cat. The mammal landed back on the bed, letting out a terrible yowl. One of the creature's legs struck the jar and we were flying again, this time right off the bed. There was just a moment's breath-stopping freefall, and then the whole world was nothing but the din of shattering glass. The jar had smashed open.

We were free! Velma looked uninjured, and I was feeling OK, under the circumstances. One last yowl cut through the air. I saw the cat's tail disappear through the crack in the door. Maybe that cat wasn't so dumb? It knew better than to stick around and take the rap for this accident when the Boy came back. I was only sorry there had been no time to say thanks to Netta.

That was OK. We had other things on our mind. Chances were strong that the Humans had heard the sound of breaking glass. We had to move fast before one of them got here.

'We need to get Jake,' said Velma.

The grasshopper would have done it too, but I sensed this was a time to play smart. 'There's no time. The Boy'll be here any second now. We've got to come back with reinforcements.'

The thump of footsteps from outside the room helped Velma make up her mind. We both raced towards the door before the Boy burst back in.

As the huge door swung open, we raced through the crack and out onto the landing. The Boy's giant clod-hopping feet just missed us as it raced into the room.

'There's an open window this way,' I said. We ran and hopped back along the landing at top speed.

When we reached the doorway, I turned to the grasshopper. 'You go!' I said. 'Go and get the Professor. Bring him to the House as fast as you can.'

'Where are you going to be, Bug?'

'The Cellar.'

The grasshopper knew I would have explained if there'd been time. There wasn't. Velma half-hopped, half-flew up to the window ledge. She looked back at me once.

'You'll have to move it,' I shouted, 'but be careful, Velma—there are robber flies in those woods.'

There—I'd gone and said it. Velma speared me with that look of hers. She didn't say anything, but I got the message. Velma was one tough grasshopper.

'OK, OK,' I said. 'But go easy on them.'

I tried to sound confident, but a sudden fear gripped me by the thorax—would we be able to pull this off? Were we in over our heads this time? Perhaps that's why I said my next words.

'One more thing,' I shouted. 'My real name . . . it's Herbert.'

A smile flashed across Velma's face like a sliver of moon on a cloudy night. Then she leapt out of the open window.

18

I found Slade and his gang under a shelf in the Cellar. As far as I could tell, they were still working on Slade's masterplan to take over the House, the Garden, the entire known world. The cockroach was the only one talking. The whole gang was here, though Juno sat away from the group on her own. I couldn't help noticing that Slippery Pete was in the inner circle now, sitting right alongside the boss. The little silverfish didn't look too cut up about abandoning Moose, who remained further back in the ranks. The big stag beetle was doing his best to follow the conversation.

Most of the guys looked kinda surprised to see me crawling up to them. Not Slade. He looked more amused than anything. That grin was back firmly in place.

'Hey, Bug,' he began. 'I know I said don't be a stranger, but I didn't mean—'

I spared myself the end of this sentence. 'Why did you do it, Slade?'

'Ah . . . you'll have to be a little more specific, Bug.'

'Take your pick. Why did you lie about Velma? Why

did you send me and the kid upstairs when you knew Humans were in? When you knew that nutball Boy was around?'

The grin never left the cockroach's face. That grin was starting to irritate me. 'Now I remember why we called you "Bug",' he sneered. A crazy challenge danced in his eyes. 'How do you think I got where I did, Muldoon?'

'It isn't good manners to answer a question with a question, Slade. But since you asked . . . As far as I can see, you started out in the sewer. Now you forage for crumbs in a cellar. Yeah, you've sure come up in the world.'

I guess I hit a sensitive spot with that one. Slade began to get sort of agitated, though to his credit, the grin didn't slip. 'So I'm no good, is that it?' he snapped. 'Well so what? What I'm after is no worse than what anyone else wants. I'm just better at getting it, and that's because I don't kid myself about loyalty and friendship and feelings and all that garbage. That's your problem, Muldoon. You're a smart enough guy, but you buy into all that stuff.'

'I'll tell you why I lied about your precious grasshopper and why I sent you upstairs. Yeah, we knew what the Boy was up to, we knew it'd caught the grasshopper. So the kid's a psycho. It takes all sorts to make a world. I told you to head up there because what I'm doing down here is too big and too important to have a snoop like you mess it up.'

'And so you figured the Boy would take care of me like it was taking care of Velma, huh? But why didn't you just have your scorpion deal with me earlier on?' I asked. 'She could have done the job in a flash. Why trust to luck?'

'I don't trust anything or anybody!' snarled the cockroach. He cast a dark glance at Slippery Pete. 'Getting the scorpion to do what we want hasn't turned out to be quite as easy as we thought. She keeps on wanting to know the reasons for why we do every little thing.'

The cockroach made himself take a deep breath. After all (he was probably telling himself) a beetle like me posed no threat to him and his grand plans. 'To be honest, Bug,' he went on, more calmly now, 'a small-timer like you just wasn't important enough to take the risk. But I didn't want you shooting right back to your Garden and blabbing everything you knew.' Grin, grin.

'So what now, smiley?'

Slade just went on grinning, but I saw the emptiness in his eyes. Had that emptiness always been there, even in the old days, and I'd just never noticed it? One of us had changed, that was for sure.

'Well, would you like the good news or the bad news?' he asked.

'I'll take the good.' That's me, ever the optimist.

'You just moved up a league, Bug. It seems I can no longer dismiss you as a small-timer any more. Congratulations.'

'Why, thank you. I'm overcome. And the bad news?'

'The bad news is, that means it *is* worth having Juno deal with you now.'

'You're right, Slade. I've heard better news.' I wasn't exactly enjoying the cut and thrust of this little chinwag, but I had to buy some time. That's why I went on blabbing. 'So . . . you're going to have me killed in cold blood, are you, Slade?'

The cockroach shrugged. 'You can warm up, if you like. It makes no difference to me, and I'm sure it'll make no difference to Juno.' He gave the nod to Slippery Pete. The slimy little silverfish smirked as if he'd been waiting his whole life for this moment. He began to relay the message to Juno. The little creep's tail rose and twirled excitedly as he explained in the ancient tongue how I was a dangerous enemy who had to be dealt with if Juno was ever to see home again.

Slade looked me over one last time, and when he spoke it sounded a lot like he was saying his goodbyes. They weren't the sweetest I'd ever heard. 'You could have been a bigshot, Bug,' he said sadly, 'but your feelings got in the way. Show me a guy with feelings, and I'll show you a sucker. And everyone knows what happens to suckers round here . . . '

'Let me guess,' I said. 'They get a grateful pat on the back and then they're sent on their merry way, right?' I was doing my best to crack as tough as I could, but, truth is, it was getting hard. The reason why was already moving my way. The scorpion. So *this* was what happened to suckers round here . . .

'So long, Bug,' said the cockroach I had once considered my friend.

I turned to meet my fate. I didn't much like the look of it. Here's why. I've known fear. Over the years I've gone up against spiders and toads, birds and fish, wasps and robber flies. I've been scared each and every time, but you learn to control your fear. It comes with the job. But I'll tell you, I've never known fear like I did when that scorpion edged forward. Her eyes fixed on me without emotion, and suddenly I knew this was it. I couldn't trick my way out of danger this time. I couldn't hide, couldn't run away. I couldn't do anything.

I was a goner.

19

Suddenly a dark shape loomed up to one side of us.

'Now hold on a minute,' drawled a deep voice. It sounded uncertain, apologetic. 'I . . . I just don't think this is right. You know, Bug has always done OK by us.'

It was Moose! The big, beautiful stag beetle was standing up for me! He had lumbered up and was positioning himself between me and Juno. All things considered, I would rather have had something else between me and that scorpion—like maybe a forest or a small country—but Moose wasn't bad as the next best thing.

Of course, Slade didn't have time for such displays of loyalty. 'Get out of the way, you overgrown half-wit!' the cockroach screamed.

Moose stayed put.

Slippery Pete joined in. 'Don't start trying to think now!' the silverfish yelled at the stag beetle. 'Just move!'

But Moose didn't move for Pete either. The stag beetle looked sort of sorry to be causing all this trouble, but he didn't budge. Not when the little silverfish tried to reason with him, and not when the little silverfish went back to yelling.

Slade was flat out of patience. 'Tell Juno to get him out of the way!' he barked. Without a moment's hesitation for his longtime partner in the fight game, Slippery Pete translated the order to the scorpion.

Juno scuttled forward, but not too fast. Her face was impassive—a mystery—but somehow I sensed uncertainty on her part. If only I could speak to her, make her understand. She didn't show enough uncertainty, however, to stop from moving forward. Trouble had arrived and it was going to go off, big-time.

Moose held his ground, and when the scorpion reached him, he reared up as high as he could go. The fight got underway when Moose locked his antler-like jaws just under the enemy's stinger. I knew that the scorpion was incredibly strong, but Moose was no slouch in the muscle department either. It was a strain, but he held the stinger off. The fighters swayed like two sleepy dancers, only this dance was going to end in a fatality.

Meanwhile, Slade had completely abandoned his act as the smiling crime boss. It was No More Mr Nice Cockroach now. 'I thought you said you could control the big lug!' he screamed at Slippery Pete. 'Had him under your antenna, you said! Well, call the fool off!'

The little silverfish hopped around anxiously. 'C'mon, Moose, quit joking around, willya? The boss has got things to do, you're just getting in the way here . . . '

Pete kept up with that line of things, but it was pretty clear that the giant stag beetle wasn't paying much attention. No big surprise. If I'd been in his position, there's only one thing I'd have been concentrating on, and that would be the huge stinger dangling over my head. Moose was holding it at bay, but that left him wide open to the scorpion's pincers, which held him in a vice-like grip.

It didn't look as if Moose could hold on much longer, but somehow the stag beetle managed to speak. 'Sorry, Pete . . . ' he gasped, 'this . . . is one . . . fight . . . I'm not going to . . . throw!'

It was agony to stand by and watch. Every part of my exoskeleton was itching to go and help the big beetle out, but I knew there was nothing I could do. Not when I was surrounded by Slade's goons.

Their boss's anger was spiralling up to greater and greater heights. 'This is ridiculous! Tell her to finish it off!' he screamed at Slippery Pete. 'He's just a dumb beetle!'

I had thought that Moose was nearing the end, but somehow, incredibly, the big beetle seemed to draw strength from Slade's insults. Though he was held fast in the scorpion's agonizing grip, he still managed to keep the stinger from striking. I watched in awe. You had to hand it to the big stag beetle. After all those fixed matches in which Moose had thrown the fight, who'd have thought that the boy had heart?

But there's a sad truth about the fight game: heart will only get you so far, and then it all comes down to superior firepower. There was no question who had the superior firepower in this fight. It was the giant scorpion, hands down. The question wasn't *who* would win, it was *when* would Juno win?

I closed my eyes. I knew how this was going to turn out and I didn't much care for the script. It wasn't something I needed to see. For a few seconds I only heard the grunts of battle continuing. Things didn't sound good for Moose.

And then a clear, strong voice rang out across the dank air of the cellar.

'Stop right there!'

You've gotta love that Velma. I opened my eyes in time to see the grasshopper leaping down from the Cellar's broken window. Clinging to her back was an insect I knew well. The Professor! The book louse's eyes were wide open. I don't know if it was with fear or excitement or a wild cocktail of the two.

Every bug in the cellar froze at this unexpected development—even Moose and the scorpion paused in their combat, though they did not relax their fighting holds.

The Professor blinked, taking in the odd collection of gangland insects that were staring at him. Then he turned his attention to the scorpion only and began speaking. I couldn't tell you what he said. That's because I couldn't understand a single word of it. But someone could, and that someone was Juno. This was what I'd been banking on—that the language wouldn't present a problem to someone as smart as the Professor. The gamble paid off. He spoke much more fluently than the silverfish had. Now my whole plan rested on the scorpion's reaction to what the book louse was saying. As she listened, Juno slowly relaxed her grip on Moose. Her back slowly unfurled. But more amazing than that, I could see the feelings swell behind her pinprick eyes.

This was getting interesting. Of course, Slade knew he had to get this situation back under control. 'What's he saying?' he screamed.

Slippery Pete the silverfish quickly explained that the Professor was saying something about how the scorpion was being tricked, how they'd lied in order to get her to do their dirty work, how they had no intention of helping her get home, and so on. The meatballs around me shifted uneasily.

'Do something!' shrieked Slade at the silverfish. 'Tell her he's lying! Tell her to stop him!'

Pete did his best. He started to gabble something at the scorpion, but in his anxiety he wandered a little too close to me. I made my move before the insects around me could do anything. I gave the slimy little silverfish a good, old-fashioned whack on the head. *BOP!* It felt sweet, and it did the job. Slippery Pete could talk a good game, but he couldn't take a punch. The silverfish was out like a light.

A couple of roaches grabbed me, but I didn't care. It was too late now. The Professor was speaking again and I could follow the gist of what he was saying by reading the scorpion's eyes. I watched as the confusion in them turned to understanding, and then to sorrow.

And finally to anger. When the Professor had finished, the scorpion's back swept up into its lethal arc. This was something everyone could understand loud and clear— the universal language of extreme danger. Slade's boys weren't the brightest, but even they figured that now might be a good time to get the heck out of there while they still could. Suddenly there were insects whizzing off in all directions. The only ones who stayed put were Velma, the Professor, and Moose.

Of course, one insect was far ahead of the others. Slade wasn't stupid. He had begun to leg it before the rest of them. Juno ignored the others as they scurried to safety. It was Slade she was after. She ran, but the cockroach had a good head start and he was as fast as ever. Slade zipped across the Cellar floor.

'Where's he going?' asked Velma, by my side now.

'I'm not sure,' I said, 'but I know one thing. That hole he's heading for . . . that's where we saw a couple of rats not too long ago.'

Slade charged headlong into the blackness of the hole. Juno was still racing across the floor after him, but the scorpion didn't have Slade's pace. She must have realized she didn't stand a chance of catching him and she began to slow down.

I couldn't help wondering—did Slade know what he was doing? He was fast and he was smart, and I wouldn't have been too surprised to find out he had an escape route already worked out. Then again, had he simply panicked and legged it without thinking about where he was going?

As if in response to my question, I heard the sudden squeaking of the rats from beyond the far wall. What did it mean? Had Slade run right into the jaws of his enemy? Or were the rats simply expressing their frustration that the cockroach had got away? There was no way of knowing for sure.

But then suddenly there was another faint noise in the distance. Its lonely sound rattled around the Cellar.

'What's that?' asked Velma.

I listened to the frantic *TAP, TAP, TAP* of the death watch beetle a few seconds more, and I wondered if it was talking about Slade or not.

'Death is in the House,' I said.

20

There was no time for detailed explanations. Seconds counted. I shouted what I had in mind to Velma and then opened up my wing case.

This was no time to get neurotic about flying. OK, I'd had some bad in-flight experiences. My wing had been pretty torn up, and it still hurt when I was flying. I wobbled a lot in the air. Well, so what? I had to put it all behind me. I needed to get back to the Boy's room as quickly as I could, and flying was the quickest way. I began to flap like my life depended on it. It probably did, and Jake's life *certainly* did.

I flew up the stairs that led up and out of the Cellar. The door was still closed but I squeezed through the gap underneath it.

And then I was in the light of the House again. I took to the air once more, keeping an eye out for any unexpected surprises that might be lurking in this alien landscape. I didn't want to have any more unpleasant encounters with vacuum cleaners or rolled-up newspapers or anything. I felt sure that the buzz of my wings would attract the attention of a Human, but none appeared.

I flew up the next flight of stairs and along to the Boy's room. The door was open slightly, and as I approached it, I had to fight back the fear that rose inside me. Like every truly Bad Place, the Boy's room sent off wave after wave of hopelessness and violence. I flew right in there.

Bad news. The Boy was still there. It had cleared up the glass where our prison had shattered. The big question was, what else had the Human been up to? Was it too much to hope that it had simply forgotten about Jake?

I guess it was. Even as I arrived, the Boy was putting the last of the broken glass into a container. Then it started crossing the room, back towards the window where Jake had fallen. But was it too late anyway? The fly was still lying flat on his back on the ledge. His body wasn't moving. Had Shaky Jake experienced his last sugar buzz?

There wasn't time to find out. I didn't know what was going on in that sicko mammalian brain, but I knew it wasn't thoughts of universal love for every living thing. I had to do something *now*.

But what can you do when you're up against something hundreds of times bigger than you are? Something that could smush you flat with a casual flick of its hand.

I did the only thing that popped into my head. I did one loop of the room to work up speed and then flew straight at the Boy's big fleshy face. Its eyes opened wide in surprise, but I was moving fast. Before it could do anything, I hit my target, the kid's great big bulbous nose. I bit as hard as I could, then took to the air again before the Boy's hand could get to me.

It wasn't time to celebrate just yet. I feinted left, then pulled a sharp loop right. Pain stabbed through my bad wing, but I didn't have the luxury of giving in to it. I had to focus all my attention on flying better than I'd ever done before.

I knew the Boy wouldn't expect me to try and pull the same trick again, so that's exactly what I did. I flew in fast and low and hit its nose head-on. The Boy's reactions were faster now, but there was still time for my mandibles to nip at the flesh. And then I was off again, swooping under the giant hand that was swinging towards me.

I couldn't chance pulling that stunt a third time. I took to the high ground, flying up close to the ceiling. My dodgy wing was aching so badly it felt as if it was going to drop off. I knew better than to give it a rest. I remembered what happened to Jake when *he* took a breather on the ceiling.

Down below, the Boy had run over to the drawers by the bed. It soon found what it was after. The expression changed on its ugly mug and I saw all those white teeth glistening. I could see why. In one hand it held the folded comic. In the other hand it held the spray-thing it had used to bring Jake down.

Remember what I said about superior firepower? I was as outgunned now as a gossamer-winged butterfly taking on a colony of army ants. The only chance I stood was to keep on moving, to stay ahead of that deadly spray of chemicals, to dodge the lethal sweep of that comic.

I did OK for a while, but this kid was good. After a few attempts, it managed to catch me with the tail end of a spray. It wasn't a full-on hit, but enough to leave me feeling pretty groggy. It was a weird sort of tiredness, one that made every part of my body feel as heavy as stone. Just landing for a nice little rest sounded like paradise.

Keep flying! I screamed through the fog that was descending on my brain. I dropped suddenly and whizzed under the kid's bed. Maybe there would be somewhere to hide under? No luck. The kid was a neat freak—there was nothing. I would be a sitting target for the Human's bug spray under here.

I did my best to guess where the Boy would be right now, and I flew out from the opposite end of the bed. Like I said, the Boy was good. It anticipated the move and was waiting for me. As I whizzed back into the open, it caught me with a good blast full-on. *FFSSSSSSSHHHHTT!*

The stones in my limbs grew to boulders. Just staying airborne was the hardest thing I'd ever done. Even my good wing was in agony. My bad wing was screaming in protest.

I don't know how, but I stayed in the air a moment longer. It didn't do me any good. I wasn't thinking straight and, even if I *had* been, I doubt my body could have followed my brain's instructions.

I was dimly aware of the Boy's arm starting its swing, and aware too of the fact that I could do nothing to stop it. It was almost a relief when the comic hit. KA-POW! Almost, but not quite. Suddenly my world was nothing but darkness and pain and I was falling to the carpet.

I landed on my back and began to get on down to the Terminal Shuffle, just as Jake had done earlier that day. It was an effort even to open my eyes, but I forced them open.

The giant Boy was standing over me, holding the comic up high. Any second now it would come crashing down on me, and that would be the end. It didn't happen. It didn't happen because the Boy had frozen. I looked up hopefully. I'm not much of a student of mammalian communication signals, but I can recognize fear when I see it. This kid was terrified. The fear was flying off it in waves.

The only part of it that moved was the eyes. Wide open in panic, they looked down at the thing that was steadily crawling up the Boy's leg.

It was Juno! The scorpion had reached the Boy's knee, and she kept on going. Her back was arched to show off that lethal stinger to best effect. This was what I'd been waiting for. This was why I'd been trying to buy time— enough time for Velma and the Professor to explain things to Juno and then guide the scorpion up to the Boy's room.

The Human was mumbling now. I couldn't tell you what it was saying, but it didn't sound all that happy. Little drops of water—I guess they call it sweat— appeared on its forehead. They began to roll down its face, but it didn't dare lift a hand to wipe them.

That's probably because the scorpion had reached the Boy's shoulder. Juno arched her back further and further until the tip of her stinger was millimetres from the Boy's trembling ear. I got the distinct impression that this kid wanted to be anywhere else but here at this particular moment. The Boy was whacko, but it wasn't stupid. Its mind had to be doing laps round such lovely thoughts as pain and paralysis, and of course, the big D itself. You couldn't blame it. The sight of the scorpion still unleashed a deep-seated terror hard-wired into me. But as I looked at the two of them, scorpion and Human, a new thought occurred to me. I had no doubt which one was the monster, and it was the one standing on two legs.

A high-pitched scraping sound drew our attention to the other side of the room. The insect who had made the noise was on the table top, next to a stretch of white wall. Velma. The Professor crouched beside her, and behind them was another insect, a big one. I was glad that Moose had decided to join the party.

OK, it was show time. None of us knew if this would work or not, but we had to give it a try. The grasshopper began once again to spit out that protective foam of hers. Its rusty colour stood out clearly against the white walls.

When there was enough of the foam to work with, Velma stretched up and began to move it into patterns on the wall.

The book louse called out instructions while Velma carefully made these odd squiggly shapes on the wall. Each one was nearly as big as the grasshopper herself. I guess it's something Human's call writing—each squiggle represents a sound, or something like that, and when you put them together, you make a word. It strikes me as an unnecessarily complicated system, but I wasn't complaining. I watched as the line of squiggles grew longer.

I heard later that the Professor really wanted to put up a quotation by some Human or other. He felt that it captured exactly what we needed to say. But Velma, who only had a limited supply of spit, told him to keep it short and sweet. Here's what appeared on the wall in dripping red:

STOP

The Boy was trembling like crazy now. I wasn't sorry. This kid had been happy enough to dole out the fear and suffering. It was time it learned an important lesson—what goes around, comes around.

The scorpion pulled back her stinger a little, giving the Boy space to nod its head. It did so jerkily. Then its eyes did this weird little flutter and the Boy fell to the floor. The Professor explained later that this is a self-defence mechanism called fainting. Doesn't look like much of a means of defence to me, but there you go.

As the Boy fell into a crumpled heap, the scorpion hopped off it and landed neatly on the table top. She was a whole lot nimbler than I expected. She and Moose wasted no time. They started tipping over the remaining jars to set free the other prisoners on Death Row. The room was filled with the sound of smashing glass.

The effects of the chemicals were wearing off me. That, or the events of the last few minutes had done wonders to pep me up. I was up and moving towards the window ledge to check out Shaky Jake. The housefly was still flat on his back. Was Jake another victim of the bug killer lying on the floor? If Jake was dead, our victory was meaningless.

As I got nearer, I thought I could hear a faint *TAP, TAP, TAP*. Panic squeezed me like the pincers of a scorpion. Not Jake too! The fly couldn't be dea—

It wasn't the drumming of the death watch beetle I could hear. It was Shaky Jake smacking his mouth-tube hungrily. His compound eyes met mine.

'Hey, B-Bug,' said the fly weakly. 'Got any s-s-s-sugar?'

21

Velma wasted no time. This was a big story and she had the scoop on it. A couple of days after it all happened, the grasshopper was frantically polishing up her account before broadcasting it across the Garden. At one point she paused and asked me how I knew that the plan would work.

'I didn't,' I told her.

'You mean you gambled everything on a guess?'

'It was kind of an educated guess. See, every time that silverfish was talking to the scorpion, I noticed his tail would twirl like crazy. That's how I knew they were lying to her. I just reckoned that if we could just find a way of telling her the truth . . . '

'But you didn't know how Juno would react?'

'Who knows how anyone's going to react to the truth?' I answered. 'Gut feeling. Sometimes that's all there is to go on.'

Velma shook her head in amused wonder. 'Pretty slick,' she said.

'I have moments.'

I left her to meet her deadline. I had an appointment to

keep over by the House. I had a lot on my mind as I walked over. I've said goodbye to a lot of insects in my time, but I can never get used to saying it to friends. That's tough, because here I was again, polishing up my goodbyes.

The Professor was waiting near the corner of the House. It was my first time back this way since the business with the Boy. It felt weird being here, but I knew there was no danger now. After our little warning, the Boy hadn't harmed another insect. In fact, it had stayed in its room from that time on. It and the Woman—the one with the lethal vacuum cleaner—had left earlier today. It didn't look as if they were coming back. The visit was over. The monster was gone. It had rained as they left—somehow that seemed appropriate. The real killer in the rain was gone.

I could tell the Professor was pleased that I'd rolled up to send him off.

'I knew you wouldn't let us go without wishing *bon voyage,* Bug, m'boy,' he began. The Professor was nervous and excited. He had good reason to be—he was taking on a pretty big job here, travelling with Juno to help her get back home.

I'd been shocked at first, but the Prof explained it like this—he'd done a lot of reading and he'd done a lot of thinking. Now it was time to get out into the world and see what answers were hiding there. He'd gone on about the quest for knowledge and truth and all that. I'm sure he believed it too. Me, I think that wasn't the whole reason. Deep down he'd been getting pretty bored under that log of his. The action in the cellar had given him a taste of something he'd never known before, a bit of excitement and adventure. I reckon part of him was looking for more of the same.

'Velma couldn't come to see you off,' I explained. 'She said to say sorry.'

'Yes, yes, of course,' said the Professor. I guess he was a little sad, but he hid it well. 'And Jake?'

'Still recuperating. He went to stay with a cousin of his down on the farm. Right about now he's probably sitting on a cow pat and enjoying the sunshine.'

'Good, good,' said the book louse. 'Splendid. For a common housefly, he is indeed quite uncommon.'

When she heard our voices, Juno crept slowly out from her hiding place behind the rubbish bin. I nodded to her. The giant scorpion nodded back. It wasn't much as communication went, but it was better than nothing. It was a whole lot better than communicating with that stinger of hers.

Nerves were making the Professor ramble on even more than usual. 'Well now, all that remains is for our travelling companion to arrive and we shall be on our merry way, I do believe.'

This was news to me. 'Travelling companion? Who's going with you?'

The answer came from behind me. I'd know that deep, slow drawl anywhere.

'It was time for me to make a career move,' said Moose. The big stag beetle joined us. 'You know, with Slade gone . . . and then Slippery Pete doing a runner.'

'Has anyone heard where he went?' I asked. Moose shook his head. I wasted half a second wondering what had happened to the creepy little silverfish. A guy like that would always find some new angle for re-entering the world of crime, I knew it. Bugs like him always seem to land on their six feet.

The stag beetle went on. 'I was starting to think my heart wasn't in the fight game anyway. A change of location sounded like a good thing. So when the Professor asked me to come along, I said yes.'

'Speaking of which, we really must be off,' said the

Professor. 'When one is going halfway around the planet, one really shouldn't dilly-dally at the outset, eh, my boy?'

He continued rattling on about the planet and all that, and I sort of knew what he meant. There are some insects who say that we're all of us living on this giant ball of earth, bigger than anything you could imagine. Big enough for a million Gardens.

Who knew if it was true? One thing's for sure—there's an awful lot of world out there. Whether they made it to their destination or not, I knew we wouldn't be seeing the three of them again.

Suddenly Juno spoke. Her voice was surprisingly gentle. For the first time, I found myself wondering who and what she had left behind at home, wherever home might be. What about friends? Family? The scorpion kept her eyes on me as she spoke, then she turned to the book louse to provide the translation.

'What did she say?' I asked the Professor.

'She says she'd like to give you a great big hug goodbye.'

I took one look at those giant deadly pincers. They could crush me in a second. My thoughts must have been stamped right across my mug. 'Well, I . . . I—' I began.

The scorpion let out a short laugh and said something else.

'She says it was a joke,' translated the Professor.

I played along and pulled out a smile. You can always rely on deadly tropical arachnids for that humorous touch. By way of changing the subject, I asked the Professor something that had been on my mind.

'You said that what you really wanted to write on that Boy's wall was some quotation, right? I've been wondering what it was.'

'Yes, yes,' said the Professor. 'You'd be surprised at what the Human species is capable of.' I remembered what the Prof had told me about the purpose of the Boy's tray full of insects—was the book louse right in thinking that the Human was pursuing knowledge and nothing else? It was a tough call. I'm not sure the Boy itself would have been able to tell.

'So the quotation?' I prompted.

'Ah, Blake, my boy,' declared the Professor, not making much sense to me. 'Yes, yes—what I had in mind was—' He cleared his throat to deliver the lines with due emphasis:

> 'Kill not the moth, nor butterfly
> For the Last Judgment draweth nigh.'

I didn't know exactly what it meant, but I got the gist. It was plenty.

'And you're saying a Human wrote that?'

The Professor nodded vigorously.

'Then I guess maybe they're not all so bad,' I said.

This was pretty high-flying stuff where I come from, and Moose didn't have too much to contribute to a conversation on literature and inter-species ethics. But he was keen to say his goodbyes too.

'So long, Bug,' drawled the giant stag beetle.

'So long, pal.'

'Yes, yes, goodbye, Bug, m'boy, and thank you for every—'

Professional modesty forced me to cut the book louse off. 'Yeah, yeah, just keep workin' on those Big Questions, huh, Prof?'

And then they set off. I watched them make their way slowly along the driveway. Before they turned the corner, they looked back and gave one final wave. I didn't want to go all mushy, so I kept it brief.

'Good luck,' I called. And then the three of them were gone forever.

Epilogue

Death can take a lot of forms in a Garden like this, and not many of them are going to win any popularity contests. But today was different. For one day in the whole long, hard year, nobody minded Death coming around. Just this once, we welcomed it. On MayDay, Death was a celebration.

Different rules applied in the Garden on MayDay. The morning was a time of waiting. It seemed as if everyone in the Garden was casting eager glances over at the pond, where the mayfly nymphs were nearing the end of their long aquatic wait. The sun seemed to take forever to crawl up to its zenith.

By early afternoon the party had begun. The mayfly nymphs were nymphs no more. Their cases had split open on the surface of the water and winged insects had emerged. Each one rested a while on the grass before going through the final moult.

Then it was time for the mayflies to take to the air. Soon it was full of them. They were everywhere, thousands of them, great swirling black clouds of mayflies. They danced and sang and swooped and partied across the whole Garden. They danced and flew as if there was no tomorrow.

Sure. For the mayflies there *was* no tomorrow. This was it for them. Month after month as underwater larvae had led up to this one hot day and this one day alone. MayDay was the only day they would live as adult mayflies. You've gotta believe they packed a lot into it.

As adults they didn't even have mouths to eat with. No stomachs to digest food. What was the point? There was just time to give themselves up to glorious flight. Just time to have one slam-bang, first and last blow-out of an airborne party, so it had better be a good one.

It was.

The party atmosphere rolled out over the whole Garden. On MayDay everyone took a break. There would be plenty of time tomorrow for the daily round of trying to eat or not be eaten. For now everyone just relaxed and enjoyed the festivities.

Dixie had ordered his boys to pull back the cover of rhubarb leaves that hung over the bar. That way the regular patrons could sit and enjoy the party while sipping some of Dixie's extra-reserve honeydew—the good stuff he usually keeps in the back. Drinks were half-price in honour of the holiday. (I'd suggested to Dixie that drinks be on the house. The fat slug just laughed. MayDay is MayDay, but business is business.)

We didn't mind. We just sat back and enjoyed the show. I turned and gave Velma what I thought was my most charming smile. That smile doesn't let me down too often but Velma is one tough nut.

'What's with you?' said the grasshopper.

What could I say? Like the thousands of bugs swirling across the skies above us, thoughts were swirling around my head. I was wondering how different any of us in the Garden were from the mayflies. Like the death watch beetle said, we were all heading to the same place in the end. How long did we get to play in the sun before we got chomped or smushed, or smushed and *then* chomped? I knew not even all of the Professor's deep thinking under a dark log could turn up an answer to that one.

I'm no philosopher, but here's my take on the whole 'What's the point of it all?' thing: life in the Garden is kinda like that old joke about the food you hear from time to time in Dixie's bar. You know the one. 'How's the food?' goes the question. And the answer is, 'Terrible and, what's more, there isn't enough of it.'

Life in this Garden could be terrible too, but there could never be enough. You had to fight for every minute of it, all the while knowing it could end at any time. But, unlike the mayflies, none of us knew exactly when or how that might happen. Not Jake, always in search of the next chunk of sugar. Not Netta, reunited with her crew and living aboard a new ship full of blood. Not Moose or the Professor or Juno, setting off on the longest journey of their lives and each looking for something different at journey's end. Not even my good friend Velma.

And not me either—yours truly, Bug Muldoon.

These weren't the most pleasant thoughts—not the kind you want to offer up as party chit-chat on MayDay, at any rate. But the funny part was, I wasn't feeling down about it or anything. In fact, things were looking pretty clear to me for once. You've just got to work out what's important for you in life, I reckon, and then stick by it. That was the trick of it. The world was a brutal place, no doubt about it, but that meant it was all the more important to stick by your friends.

That's all good and well, but how could you put it into words without coming off sorta goofy? I didn't try. I just said, 'Happy MayDay, Velma.'

The grasshopper snorted with laughter, like she knew what I'd been thinking. I wouldn't put it past her. 'Yeah, right. Happy MayDay . . . Herbert.'

Her multi-faceted eyes twinkled, and above our heads the mayflies danced like a million shooting stars.

Also by Paul Shipton

Bug Muldoon and the Garden of Fear
ISBN 0 19 271645 X

'The name's Muldoon—Bug Muldoon, I'm a private investigator. I'm working on a missing-insect case. It's nothing special. But in my line of work, you take whatever you're offered. It pays the rent.

It's the case of Eddie the Earwig. He used to run around with a rough crowd—a lot of his friends were wasps. And now he's gone missing.

But that's not all. There's some pretty weird stuff going on in the Garden. Lots of other insects have gone missing. The ants are doing jazz-dances. The Wasp Queen is threatening to kill me. And the Spider has me marked down for supper.

I'm starting to get a very bad feeling about all this . . . '

'Just a huge, huge bundle of fun . . . full of that wacky humour that really appeals to children . . . the animals are wonderful! I couldn't put it down . . . I liked it enormously—it goes for a big age range—anything from 8 to 13.'

Treasure Islands (BBC Radio 4)

The Mighty Skink

ISBN 0 19 271488 0

Long, long ago, when the World Forest was young, all the animals lived together. But many of the animals wanted to hunt and devour the monkey. Man, who was first and best and wisest of animals, took pity on the monkey. He built The Fence and filled it with Electricity. Then he placed the monkey inside The Fence and decreed that we were never to leave.

So goes the Tale. But when Skink, a monkey new to the Enclosure, challenges the old wisdom, Giz decides to go and see for himself and find the answer to the Big Question: *'What's it like out there . . . out in the land of humans?'*

'This powerful, thought-provoking story is a challenging read. It takes a stark look at the role of animals in society. A beautiful, tightly written story which is very moving.'

School Librarian

'Paul Shipton's story deserves a wide readership.'

Junior Bookshelf

The Man Who Was Hate
ISBN 0 19 271814 2

Down in the darkness something stirs, and from its dreamlike wonderings one thought begins to take form, and the thought is this: It is time . . .

Victor Grundy has been chosen to help the Sleeper awake; chosen because he knows how to hate. And in return the Sleeper will destroy the people on Grundy's List, all those who have slighted or let him down over the years—and Grundy never forgets an insult. But the Sleeper has a greater destiny to fulfil and it seems that the only people who realize what is going to happen are Hope and Danny. But how can two frightened teenagers stop the evil force that will lead to the destruction of the whole world?

From: Bug Muldoon and the Garden of Fear

You may not think there's much difference between
wasps and bees. After all, they're both yellow and black,
they both buzz around the garden, they can both sting.
Well, let me tell you, there's a big difference. Bees are
mostly friendly, in a scatterbrained way. But wasps . . .
they're something different. A wasp will sting you soon
as look at you. They're mean and dangerous.

There's another difference between the two. Bees are
built to drink the nectar in flowers: they guzzle it and
then they weave their way contentedly home to the hive,
their bellies coated with pollen. Wasps, on the other
hand, are designed for eating and chewing. They feed on
other insects, fruit—stuff like that. But they do have a
fondness for nectar as well. They view it as a special
treat, and I was relying on this fact when I decided to
have my little chat with a wasp.

I selected a flower, set up my trap and waited.

And waited . . .

In my line of work you get used to waiting. It comes
with the territory. I spent the time watching the Man
from the House, who was out in the Garden pushing the

device known as a lawnmower across the grass. As I looked at him, my mind was flooded with familiar questions—*What goes on in that big mammalian brain? Is it **anything** like the way we insects think? Who are you, human? What do you think about, what do you hold dear? Do you ever see me and wonder what goes on in the mind of Bug Muldoon?*

No answers presented themselves. I went on waiting.

It was a long time before a wasp appeared. I heard its buzz first—a low angry sound that I could just make out over the whirr of the Human's lawnmower. That wasp's buzz was the sound of trouble, except if there was any trouble today I was planning on being the one to dish it out.

The buzzing stopped. I peeked out from under my leaf cover, careful not to let my head show. The wasp had landed on a flower a few feet away. It began working its way inside the flower to get at the nectar within. I heard its greedy slurp.

After a few seconds the wasp was in the air again. Its buzzing filled my ears. *Come on*, I willed it, *come to this flower—lots of nice nectar here—come to this one.*

My luck was in. The wasp hovered a moment longer, then its hum grew louder as it flew towards the flower right above me—the flower I had specially prepared. I looked up and saw its yellow-and-black body through the petals above. I waited until it was right within the flower, then I tugged hard on the vine I had threaded through the flower. The petals pulled shut around the wasp.

It was stuck.

I secured the trap and gave the wasp a few minutes to realize the predicament it was in. Its buzzing grew angrier and angrier as it tried to escape. I found the noise strangely relaxing.

At last I climbed up the stalk and spoke to where its head was.

'Comfortable enough in there?' I asked. I'm friendly that way.

'Who is this?' rasped the wasp. 'How dare you! Let me out!' He said some other stuff as well, but I don't think I should repeat language like that here.

When he was done, I asked, 'What do you know about a secret organization of ants?'

The wasp's answer was again unrepeatable.

I smiled. 'I hope you don't talk that way back home in the Wasps' Nest,' I said. 'OK, try this one—why was a squadron of wasps searching for an ant by the name of Clarissa? An ant with a white mark on her head?'

The same reply.

I wasn't getting far. I decided to let him cool off for a while, so I took a walk. A nice long walk. Maybe he'd be more talkative after that.

I wandered back to my office to check if Velma or Jake had left any messages in the soil. They hadn't. But as I was walking away from my office, I couldn't shake the feeling that something was different. Suddenly it clicked: normally I can't leave the office without Billy the caterpillar pestering me. But today there was no eager cry of 'Hey, Bug!' There was no sound at all.

I looked around anxiously, hoping the magpie hadn't returned to finish the breakfast I had so rudely interrupted the day before.

Then I saw it. Billy was not dead, but he *was* gone for ever. His life as a caterpillar was over.

He hung upside down from the stem of a plant over in the nettle patch. He was dead to the world, for he had entered the chrysalis phase. He would stay that way for a few weeks while his body reconstructed itself. When it was over, he would emerge into the sunshine as an entirely new creature, a butterfly. Just imagine—you go to sleep a caterpillar and you wake up as a butterfly! How can a creature be two such different things within one lifetime? Beats me.

Of course, after metamorphosis an insect remembers nothing of its former life. Me, I have no memories of when I was a larva. And Billy would remember nothing of his life as a caterpillar, nothing of his wild ambitions to be a private detective. He would remember nothing of me.

I took a last look at Billy, and I was filled with a terrible unease. This stinking Garden was already dangerous enough for little guys like Billy. And now things were getting worse—this case I was working on was big. Something bad was going on in the Garden— something that made it even more dangerous for the little guys—and it was bigger than just a harmless group of ant individualists.

I knew it was my job to find out what was going on. It was time to get some answers. It was time to renew my questioning of the wasp.

When I got back to the flower-trap, a couple of hours had passed and the wasp was feeling a bit more talkative. It's funny how being trapped without food can have that effect on you.

I put on my best tough guy voice. 'OK, we'll try again. Why were you after the ant named Clarissa?'

'Ants don't have names,' snarled the wasp contemptuously from inside the trap.

'That's true,' I agreed, 'but then wasps don't get caught in flower-traps either, and yet look at you, buddy-boy.'

He didn't have an answer for that. I asked again about Clarissa, and to jog his memory this time I gave him a jab in the side.

After the twentieth time of asking, he gave in. 'We

were looking for her because she was snooping where she didn't belong, and she heard something she shouldn't have heard. She knew about the Plan . . . '

I didn't like the sound of this. 'What plan is that?'

There was a long silence. When he spoke again it was with such arrogance you would have thought that *he* was the interrogator and *I* was the prisoner. This is what the wasp said:

'The Plan that's going to sweep dirty beetles like you clean out of the Garden. That's what you are, isn't it? A dirty beetle. Well, your days are numbered, pal. The new alliance between wasps and ants will destroy everything that gets in its way. The Garden is on the threshold of a new era . . . '

It was a cute speech, but I couldn't help butting in. 'The Ant-Queen'll never go along with that.' Everyone knew that the Queen had little time for the wasps. I couldn't believe that she would form an alliance with them. The wasp had to be bluffing.

But what it said next sent shivers through my exoskeleton. 'Maybe the Ant-Queen's days are numbered,' he gloated.

I was about to demand what he meant, but right then my luck ran out. A squadron of wasps buzzed into view. There were five of them, flying low across the grass in an attack formation, and they had spotted me. They didn't look like they wanted a friendly chat, and they were coming this way . . .

I was back in that familiar place—deep, deep trouble.

* * *

Like most beetles I can fly, but I'm not very good. I can't compare with the great insect aviators like flies and bees, so I prefer to keep all six legs on the ground. However, I knew I had got no chance of escaping the squadron of wasps on foot.

I scuttled forward, opened my wings and took to the air. The five wasps fell into a new formation for pursuit. I zigzagged right and left, flying low over the lawn. That didn't shake them off at all. In fact, they were gaining on me.

I started climbing high, riding the warm air currents of the summer sunshine, then swooping low again. Still no luck: the wasps were more accomplished flyers than me by far. They weren't even straining, while I was flapping my wings with more and more desperation. And all the while I could hear the ominous buzz behind me, getting closer second by second.

I banked left, and flew into the shade of the apple tree. I thought maybe I could lose them in there. I looped and circled the leaves and branches, zipping in and out. When I thought I was out of sight I plummeted down to the ground. Maybe I could hide out for a while? Several apples had fallen from the tree. One of them had gone beyond ripe—it was rotten. *Perfect.*

I rushed up to it and pushed my way through the puckered brown skin of the fruit. I figured it would be a good place to hide out (even if it didn't smell too good). I worked my way right inside the squishy flesh of the apple, and listened to the wasps circling above. They sounded puzzled, they didn't know where I had gone. That suited me just fine. I let out a sigh of relief.

I shouldn't have. Something within the clammy darkness of the apple pushed its little head right up to mine, and shouted, 'OY! This is my apple! Clear off and find your own!'

It was a maggot. It must have been happily munching its way through the apple, when I had so rudely shown up.

'Listen,' I whispered. 'I just want to hang out for a couple of minutes. I won't eat anything. I don't even like apples.'

'Well, that may be so,' bellowed the maggot, 'but you can just find another apple to hang out in, can't you, buster!'

For a little maggot his voice was impressively loud. I heard the wasps' buzz get nearer.

'Keep it down, buddy,' I hissed.

'Oh, keep it down, is it?' roared the maggot. 'Well, let me tell you something, Mr-Keep-it-down. This is my apple, and I shall be as loud as I like.' Then he began to shout in a deafening sing-song, 'LA, LA, LA . . . LA, LA, LA . . . loud enough for you? . . . LA, LA, LA . . . '

I was about to reach out and shut the little twerp up—nothing permanent, you understand—but before I got to him he wriggled up and stuck his head out through the top of the apple skin. 'LA, LA, LA,' he continued to shout, 'INTRUDER IN THE APPLE! LA, LA, LA!'

I heard one of the wasps cry out, 'Down there!'

Damn! I backed up out of the apple, shook the apple gunk from my body, then glanced upwards. The wasps were hurtling down towards me in a blur of black and yellow.

I unsheathed my wings and took to the air once more. I was getting tired. My body is too heavy for my little wings, and they were feeling the strain by now. But I couldn't slow down—not when the wasps were so close.

I was approaching the pond now—the home of the big old carp that had tried to turn me into supper yesterday. As I flew over the water, I could see the massive golden bulk of the fish below. The beginnings of a plan seeped into my brain.

It was time to do something about these wasps.

I flew low over the surface of the pond and slowed my

speed right down. One of the wasps detached himself from the squadron and went into a dive. His plan, I suppose, was to swoop down from above, grab me in mid-air and carry me off.

I continued flying as slowly as possible, like I was on an afternoon joy-flight—the wasp continued to plummet, it was almost upon me, two seconds, one second . . . at the last moment I swerved sideways. I felt the wasp brush past me, as it shot downwards like a bullet, straight into the waters below. The last thing I heard was a surprised 'ERK?' before it disappeared into the water. PLOP!

I didn't stick around to see if the carp managed to get the wasp. I flew off at top speed again. *One down, four to go.* But I knew they wouldn't fall for such a simple trick a second time. What could I do now?

Then it struck me. The Man from the House was still plodding up and down the grass, pushing his lawnmower. I knew what I had to do. It was crazy, but it was my only chance.

I turned right and flew flat-out for the Man. The wasps were so close to me now they could almost reach out and grab my back legs. Almost, but not quite. The air was filled with the din of their furious buzzing, and my head was filled with the thought of their deadly stings.

I altered my flight path so that I was on a head-on collision course with the Man. Suddenly, I swooped low, straight for the mower itself. The wasps followed, hot on my tail. The metal casing of the lawnmower loomed in front of me, it filled my field of vision. I raced through the spray of cut grass, and straight on—straight towards the whirring blades of the lawnmower.

I shot through a gap between two of the blades, adjusted my angle of elevation a touch, then shot out through a second gap between the blades at the back of the mower. It was an act of precision flying.

As I soared up into the air once more, I couldn't help sneaking a look behind me. All four wasps had followed me into the path of the lawnmower. Only two emerged on the other side. The other two had not been skilful or lucky enough to avoid getting mangled by the blades.

That was three down, but there were still two to go and I was close to exhaustion. I couldn't fly much further, and the two wasps behind me sounded fresher and angrier than ever.

I was slowing down. I urged myself to push on, to fly faster, but it was no good. The inevitable happened. Two pairs of legs grabbed hold of me—one on either side. The game was up—escape was impossible. The wasps had me.

I stopped flapping, and told myself to enjoy the ride as they carried me off towards their nest. A single thought pounded through my brain: *there has to be a better way of earning a living than this . . .*